THE ZONE

#2

BLIND FIRE

Books by James Rouch

The Zone Series
#1: Hard Target
#2: Blind Fire
#3: Hunter Killer
#4: Sky Strike
#5: Overkill
#6: Plague Bomb
#7: Killing Ground
#8: Civilian Slaughter
#9: Body Count
#10: Death March

World War II Collection
#1: The War Machines
#2: Tiger
#3: Gateway to Hell

THE ZONE

#2

BLIND FIRE

James Rouch

SPEAKING VOLUMES, LLC

NAPLES, FLORIDA

2012

THE ZONE

BLIND FIRE #2

ISBN 978-1-61232-905-5

For Nora and Jim Mullee

The Zone - Central Sector

The Third Battle of Frankfurt is now into its second week, with Russian and Hungarian divisions poised to take Aschaffenburg. All civilians living south-east of autobahn A683 between Darmstadt and Offenbach have been warned to prepare for evacuation. There will only be four hours' notice of it becoming a free-fire area.

Russian casualties since the beginning of the battle are put at 27,000, with 685 tanks and other armoured vehicles destroyed. NATO losses have not been announced, but are said to be "heavy."

Twenty-seven people died, including five riot police, during disturbances at the University of Stuttgart. It is thought more bodies will be recovered when the gutted city hall is searched. It had been occupied by students protesting at the ending of exemptions and deferments for military service. The cause of the fire has not yet been established.

Since the beginning of the month. Russian advances in the central sector have added a further nineteen hundred square miles to the Zone.

The West German government has protested strongly to the NATO Supreme Commander over the decision to withdraw from Aalen without prior consultation, and the subsequent use of nuclear demolition devices thought to have severely damaged more than half the town. Triggered to catch the Russian 8th Guards Army on its entry, first reports put enemy losses at more than 20,000. A revised figure of seven to eight hundred has now been admitted.

CHAPTER ONE

"They drove straight through us, like we weren't there." The battalion commander pushed aside the fussing hands of a corpsman attempting to apply a dressing to the gaping wound in his shoulder, almost dropping the handset.

"Yeah . . . yeah, I'm OK . . ." His hand left red smears on the drab lump of plastic as he held it closer. ". . . It's that Russian column you'd better worry about: came out of nowhere, blew our minefields apart and chopped my headquarters company to pieces. We threw everything we had, knocked out a couple of T84s and an APC, but the rest just kept right on going."

Smoke, thick and black, drifted from the smashed and burning vehicles littering the roadside. The acrid fumes from the blazing tyres and ammunition forced a cough from the officer, and the involuntary action brought a spurt of blood from his wound. Again he had to hold off the hovering attendant.

"You're losing a lot of blood, sir." The medic persisted.

"So are others. Go help them, see to me later." As the corpsman moved away, the officer was forced by growing weakness first to slump against the fragment-riddled side of his command vehicle, then to slide down its armour until he sat on the muddy, oil-coloured road beside the salvaged radio pack. The light rain was washing the stains from his hands and face, spreading them on to his jacket.

"Yeah, I'm still here." Where the hell did the clown on the other end think he'd be? His concentration had to compete with a swimming sensation inside his head and an overpowering feeling of strangely detached giddiness. It wasn't unpleasant, rather like the early stages of inebriation. ". . . There wasn't much time for counting . . . I reckon about twenty-five of the Reds' latest tanks, plus an assortment of APCs, self-propelled artillery, flak and some fancy engineers wagons. Maybe forty, forty-five pieces of armour in all."

It was becoming more difficult to concentrate on the words in his ear, harder to grasp their meaning. His gaze wandered to the crushed jeep in the centre of the road. Lying there, like a carelessly tossed cut-out, it looked unreal. What little was visible of the grotesquely flattened human form among the metalwork added absurdity, not horror.

"What? . . . Say it again . . . I didn't catch . . . no nothing. The only thing between that Ruskie regiment and Frankfurt, is half a dozen small depots that couldn't muster more than ten clerks and fifty pioneers between them. If the Reds keep up that pace, you'll have them coming in by the back door in about five hours . . . that's right, five, f-i-v-e hours."

The rain made no difference to the rubber and diesel fuel-fed fires. Across the road, the turret hatches of a Soviet T84 clattered up and down, as flames and roasting gases boiled from its furnace-like interior. Rain falling on the hull rose back into the air as steam, almost before contact.

Damn it. That voice was still nagging away at him. What the hell did it want now? ". . . Cut it off with what? Even if we could catch it, the best we could do would be to bite its tail. You want to stop that commie column—you got to chop off its head. All I can do is gather together what I've got left and try to prevent any more breakthroughs, make sure it doesn't get reinforced."

He looked up. Mixed with the falling rain that felt so good on his face was a mass of floating particles of lampblack from the burning tyres. The handset felt heavy, he wished he could use his other hand to help support it.

". . . I've got ten tenths . . . that column's got cloud umbrella all the way. The Reds have picked a good day for a drive . . . Yeah, OK. I'll give you a status as soon as we get sorted out. Do what you can to stir up Casevac will you, I've got more than thirty stretcher cases that need help real bad. Yeah . . . out."

He didn't bother to secure the radio, just let the handset fall as his arm flopped to his side. Maybe it'd be a good idea to get patched up now. Funny, he'd been hit before and had felt a lot more pain from wounds that didn't look half as ugly as this one. The tumbling piece of shell casing had made a big hole, the torn edges of the material around it had been dragged in and were buried in the mangled tissue.

Still, whatever his problems, all this was nothing compared to what the poor SOBs who'd have to stop that Russian column would be letting themselves in for.

The floor of the old Chinook was smothered in mud, and its spar-ribbed walls and ceiling in tattered centrefolds and pages torn from *Hustlers* and *Playbirds*. Eddies of the slipstream coming in through an open window caused some of them to flutter and pulsate obscenely.

"Get your hairy paws off. Go buy your own."

Dooley paused in the act of detaching a bent over crotchshot from a bulkhead. He feigned disinterest as the co-pilot continued to eye him suspiciously. "Just seeing if she was a natural blonde." With a last lingering look at the model's vibrator-filled rear, he sauntered to the far end of the cabin. A brief turbulence caused him to stagger and almost lose balance. He had to grab at one of the loaded pallets.

"Sit down, you big lump. You go flying out a window and the civies down there are going to think a nuke's been dropped on them." Sergeant Hyde looked out. The suburbs of Frankfurt were behind them now, and they were just crossing the autobahn to the east of Hanau. Only a couple of the other members of the squad were visible in the equipment and stores filled interior, apart from Dooley, who sat morosely eyeing the extensive collection of soft porn from the top of a stack of ammunition boxes.

Libby sat by himself as usual, contemplating but not seeing the upside down stencilling on a case of anti-tank mines. Further away Burke could just be seen. He'd made a little cocoon for himself among the crates and was fast asleep.

At fifteen hundred feet the twin rotors of the elderly transport helicopter chopped through the passing wisps of the lowest clouds. The Chinook banked slightly as it turned on to a new heading.

Hyde's burn-scarred mask looked up as Major Revell came back from the flight deck. "Do we have a fix on those Ruskies yet?" He added nothing to the question. Since the time he'd learnt he and his section were to stay with the American outfit, the sergeant had made up his mind to treat the Yank officer with cold civility. Revell, for his part, appeared unbothered, and that irritated Hyde. All he wanted was out—to get back to his own battalion, or any British unit. Anything was better than being attached to this rag-bag squad, being treated with contempt or ignored by every Command in whose area they operated, until there was a really dirty job to do. Christ, they even had an ex-East German border guard among them, one of the despised Grepos, and the girl . . .

"No location as yet. I've told the pilot to do a wide sweep, so we come up behind their last known position. I'd rather we tracked them than suddenly found ourselves flying over them, a target for the mass of SAMs and flak they've got."

"And when we do find them, what then? Hop on ahead and set up an ambush?"

"That's about it. The orders say we stall them, and

keep on stalling them while the Staff try to scrape together a blocking force that can finish them off."

Corporal Cohen staggered back to join them. The twin chevrons on his sleeve were still clean and bright against his soiled and faded jacket. There were new contours to the bulging pockets in the flak-jacket he wore, evidence of shrewd deals with the chopper's crew. "I just got word, Major. We can have an ECM platform tasked to us within fifteen minutes of finding the Reds." He sat down heavily and fanned himself with his clipboard. His pallid features confirmed that his most recent travel sickness cure was ineffective.

He wasn't capable of expression, but Sergeant Hyde snorted his disgust. "One unarmed aircraft, stooging about overhead, doing a spot of jamming. Is that the best they can come up with?"

"Well it's better than nothing." Revell watched the rotor-blade misted rain travelling in horizontal lines across the window. "It'll stop the Ruskies squawking for close air support, and if the crew of that jammer are any good, maybe they can even screw up the column's short-range sets, force them to close up on the road."

Hyde brightened at the prospect of the target that would present. Bloody hell, he'd had little enough to feel happy about since he'd been roped in with Revell. The Yank wasn't like any officer he'd ever known, you could never tell when he was making a bleeding suggestion and when he was giving an order. It kept Hyde on edge; he'd have been happier with an officer who kept a bit of distance. You knew where you stood then.

14

Revell jotted a signal on the radio-man's clip-board. "OK, send that acknowledgement and arrange for one frequency to be left open. Have it confirmed by whoever's tasking the ECM mission. Electronic countermeasures are fine, so long as they don't blanket us as well, And keep trying for that promise of air-support. Tell them anything will do. Hot air balloons, a couple of hang gliders, any-thing."

"I'll try, Major, but I'm getting the same answer every time. Everything with wings or rotors apart from this old rust bucket is committed to the big battle south of the city—there's nothing to spare."

"Then tell them if we can't call on air, and we're not able to hold those Ruskies on our own, there's going to be T84s competing for road space with the trams on Kaiser Strasse damned soon."

As he followed Cohen back to his improvised communication board midway down the cabin, and waited for the corporal to squeeze his small frame into the even smaller space so he could get past, Revell watched Dooley.

The big man was trying to fold a couple of sheets of glossy paper quietly. There were two gaps in the wall covering near him. Revell felt his eyes being irresistibly drawn to the succession of big breasts and glistening vaginas. There certainly were a lot of whores in the world. It was crazy, some of them had really beautiful faces. He could never understand why a woman whose looks would enable her to get anything she wanted in life should squat, open her legs and play with herself in front of a camera and, effectively, a couple of million masturbating males.

15

There were still lots of pretty girls in Frankfurt too. For the last twelve months the city had carried on virtually as normal, with the fringes of the Zone barely forty kilometres away. Now it was even closer and still an air of normality reigned. But in the last two or three weeks there had been a subtle change in the general mood. Somehow, it was as if the population was enjoying one last fling, attempting to ignore the underlying feeling of growing tension. The euphoric veneer was brittle, it would take little to crack it and release panic.

They were over the Zone now, and before going forward, the major looked out. There was little to betray the fact to the untrained eye. The small villages strung out along the winding roads and clustered about intersections appeared perfectly normal, as did the scattered farmsteads. The first detail that jarred was the total absence of traffic; there should have been some even on these rural roads. Careful inspection revealed other, more ugly evidence.

It was early September, yet large areas of woodland were already stripped of autumn colour and any vestige of leaf canopy. And broad swathes of land that marched across the rolling hills had a uniformly sickly yellow appearance. Less obvious were the seemingly random clusters of circles of churned bare soil. From an altitude, they looked to be the work of a demented ploughman. Revell knew better, they were the massive craters made by long-range artillery rockets. Early on in the war, this area of the Hesse had been one of the principal assembly points for the NATO counterattack that had pushed the Russian forces back beyond Fulda, almost to the East German border.

The ferocity of the Soviet chemical and conventional barrage had crippled the planned West German and American follow-up attacks. Though the Russians had been content to let the NATO troops hold the territory, its contamination had made it a hollow victory, setting the pattern for battles that were to follow, and the formation of the Zone.

When the battles spilled beyond the Zone, then it grew accordingly, spreading out to engulf the newly ravaged ground. The loss of Frankfurt, if it followed so soon after Wurzburg and Nurnberg, would be a crippling blow to morale and strengthen the re-emerging lobby in the West that believed the time had come to attempt a negotiated peace.

The rest of the squad were sitting behind the pilot's position. Kurt was pencilling additional obscenities on the black and white illustration of a mud-spattered magazine featuring women and animals. While the grossness of his drawings was almost beyond belief, Revell had to admit the Grepo did have a degree of warped talent.

As usual, Clarence and Andrea were sitting side by side, close but not quite touching. They were working together, using triangular needle files to cut tiny nicks into the sides of 5.56mm rifle rounds. The work was being done with expert precision and loving care, each converted dum-dum bullet being carefully checked before being slotted into a magazine.

"Make sure we don't take any of those back with

us." Revell counted the number of filled mags, and worked out the total of modified rounds. A sufficient number had already been finished to keep the whole squad firing on automatic for thirty seconds or more. "There's newshawks around who'd love to get something like that for the anti-war press back home. That's one load of ammunition the General Staff wouldn't like them to have."

"Only the Russians will know of them." Andrea turned her dark brown eyes to the officer. "I do not think those we hit will be in a position to make a complaint."

That was a face Revell could have looked at all day. He'd moved heaven and earth to retain her in the squad, despite the violent opposition from I-Corps, and even though keeping her had also meant keeping Kurt. Hell, he still didn't really understand why he'd done it. It wasn't as though there was anything between them. Clarence was the only one she associated with, and even their relationship seemed to be strangely a-sexual, the only visible link between them being hatred of the Russians.

But then everyone who fought the communists soon learned to loathe them; for their atrocities, their sheer barbarity. In Clarence and Andrea though, the depth of feeling went far beyond that. For them the killing of Russians was their whole life, the very essence of their existence. Clarence's score was close to two hundred. Andrea didn't keep a tally, the most important thing to her was how soon the next chance would come.

"Smoke up ahead." The pilot leant out into the aisle and called back.

18

So Andrea's next chance would come soon. Revell stepped into the cockpit. Peering through the wiper-swept glass, he looked toward the several thin pillars of black smoke that rose to the cloud base and spread beneath it.

"Better take us down as low as you can. We'll hedge-hop from now on."

"Already doing it." The pilot indicated the altimeter, steadily dropping past the thousand feet mark. "There's no armour on this bus, not even the blades." He jerked his thumb toward the Lycoming engine above their heads. "One cannot shell through them and we're gonna be aboard an olive drab carousel, going nowhere but down. You ain't expecting me to dump you right on top of the commie column are you? Cause I ain't too keen on that."

Now they were right over the source of the smoke. Below, Revell could make out the burning tanks and trucks. A bubble of flame rose from a ditched command vehicle as its fuel ignited, mushrooming in the air behind them, before the wash from the helicopter's passage scattered and dispersed it.

"Looks like those poor shits took a hammering." The co-pilot unwrapped a piece of gum and popped it into an already full mouth.

"Yeah, the babies we're looking for sure passed this way." At fifty feet the pilot levelled out, and the countryside flashed past beneath the chopper. "You ain't answered me yet, Major. I said how close? It ain't that I'm pressing, it's just that I've got kinda attached to this body of mine. I'd like to keep it in one piece for a mite longer, like 'til I kick off through

19

old age."

"Just keep us as low as you can. Give it another ten minutes at this speed and then let's take it real easy. So long as we don't overshoot, we should stay out of trouble. They'll be concentrating their radar watch forward."

A glance was enough to tell Revell that Sergeant Hyde had everything under control in the back. The British NCO had woken Burke by the simple expedient of whipping away a vital component of his nest, causing the remainder to collapse and deposit him on the floor.

The others were already gathering their equipment together. With every move that Dooley made, small squares of folded paper fluttered out of the bottom of his jacket, until he fastened it tighter. His plunder of the decorations had been extensive.

Twelve times in fifteen kilometres they flew over wrecked NATO supply trucks, and once glimpsed the blazing guard shack of a small roadside dump.

"We were pretty fast off the mark." With unconscious skill the pilot skimmed the unwieldy helicopter over the telephone wires and occasional power lines. "But those Reds must be going like bats out of hell to have got this far. They ain't being held up by anything, just smearing anybody who gets in their way."

They whirred over a lone Mack tank transporter. It looked as if it had been bulldozed off the road. A fire was growing in the cab and the bodies of its crew lay beside it.

"That fire hasn't got a hold yet. We're right on their tail." Straining to catch a glimpse of the enemy column, Revell spotted it as the Chinook banked round the side of a wooded hill. "Down, put us down."

At the shout, the pilot brought the helicopter to a virtual standstill, then let it drop fast until it hovered only a few feet off the road. "So what now, and remember, this ain't no gunship."

"There are no important intersections for about fifteen kilometres." Revell studied the map. "Then the road forks and they could go either way. Get us ahead of the column, we'll wait for them there, and in the meantime we can drop a few presents."

A loud groan from Cohen was smothered by the howl of the engines, as the chopper soared vertically into the cloud before whirling on to a fresh heading, then, nose down, began to pick up speed. "So can we go back for my stomach later?"

"Never mind your gut, get on that radio. I want that ECM platform now. The rest of you, we've got work to do." Scanning the various loads that had been hurriedly thrown aboard before their rushed departure, it was with relief that Revell saw the crate he wanted was the one nearest the rear door. "Get it ready for a drop."

A blast of cold damp air struck at them as Hyde lowered the ramp. "Are we letting the whole lot go at once, or a handful at a time?"

"We'll make four drops at irregular intervals. That'll stop them anticipating and keep them nervous. Put down a hundred at a time, on my signal." The view the major had out of the open rear of the chopper was unreal. The whole world was a uniform gray, devoid of any feature that would serve

21

as a reference point. That insubstantial wall of cloud could be a hundred yards away, or just at the end of the ramp.

Dooley used a swing of his boot to free the final reluctant catch, and the side of the case fell away to reveal the loaded racks within. "All ready, Major."

"Right, make sure they go down on the road . . ." Revell saw the puzzled expression on Dooley's face. "Well there wouldn't be any damned point in hiding the things in the fields if the Reds are barrelling straight down the road, would there? I want them nice and conspicuous."

"Funny thing war, isn't it, Sarge?" Dooley watched the officer making his way to the cockpit. "Some dumb shits back home must have spent years developing these, figuring out how to make them camouflage themselves when they're dropped. Just when they've got it right, we come along and start scattering the bloody things out in the open."

"He's not getting fucking philosophical again is he, Sarge?" Burke yawned. "The last thing I want after a rude awakening from you is a load of bleeding waffle from him."

"Just get ready to drop two racks when I tell you." They were descending again, Hyde could tell that, as he waited for the signal, by the feeling in his stomach and the colour of Corporal Cohen's face. It went from flushed pink to white to green in as many seconds, then disappeared as the radio-man ducked down, stuck his head in a paper bag and made repulsive noises while his shoulders heaved.

Suddenly they were out of the cloud and only a hundred feet above the road. Rain swept in gusts at them, stinging their eyes. The chopper levelled out and its speed fell rapidly, so that the road was no longer a blurred black ribbon. Details could be made out. The patches of old repairs, sprouting clumps of weeds, individual puddles and longer flooded stretches where neglected ditches and field drains had overflowed.

"*Now.*" Hyde's hand slapped down on Dooley's shoulder as he saw Revell wave from the cockpit.

In swift succession Dooley tripped two releases, and a pattern of bowling ball sized objects arced over the ramp and down toward the road. Some of the spheroids landed on the verges but most, prevented from bouncing and brought immediately to rest by their special ribs and fins, settled on the road.

As the Chinook disappeared into the distance the anti-tank mines sat quietly ticking, mindlessly counting the seconds to the moment when they would arm themselves. It came, and a brief tinny buzzing signalled the activation of fuses and booby trap devices.

From that moment, until they self-destructed twelve hours later, nothing was going to get past that stretch of road while they sat there.

CHAPTER TWO

"For the last twenty bloody minutes the Sarge has had me rushing about like a ruddy blue-arsed fly, lugging these fucking heavy missiles around until the sweat's pouring off me. Now he wants me to sit down in the wet grass." After aiming a savage kick at the droplet-laden seed heads, Burke squatted down beside the mortar and began unpacking rounds.

"I wouldn't worry too much if I were you." Dooley took off his helmet and wiped the rain from his face with a scrap of filthy rag. "Chances are you're not gonna live long enough to catch a cold."

"Piss off. How do you want these fused?"

Dooley considered the question. "Well there's not much fucking chance of knocking out armour with 60mm HE, so let's go for air-bursts. Might knock some bits off the flak-wagons and . . ." he grinned, ". . . besides, they look pretty."

"You all ready here?" Major Revell stood behind the two men and looked down on the gentle slope of the meadow to the stretch of road a thousand yards away.

"Checked and double checked, Major. Any Ruskie who sticks his head out of a hatch for a look-see after the action starts is going to get his ears pierced the hard way." As the officer departed, Dooley sighted again through the RCA laser rangefinder.

From the far side of a belt of defoliated woodland came the dull boom of a powerful explosion, followed by the crackling ripple of multiple mine detonations.

"Not long now." Burke rested his hand on the mortar's barrel cover. "Christ, I'm cold now. This bloody rain is going right through me."

. "What you want is something to cuddle up to, like your buddy Clarence, with his little fraulein."

"He's not my mate. The only thing we have in common is that we're British. I don't want nothing to do with that headcase. Anyway, I don't reckon there's anything between them. I've never seen him touch her."

"You've never seen me screwing, but I do it." Having wiped the rangefinder, Dooley stowed it in its compact carry case. "Nice little toy, saves a ranging shot, but when things warm up there won't be much time for pissing about with gadgets. It'll all be down to how fast we can stuff those little bastards down the tube." Dooley's broad features creased into a wide grin again. "If the shits get close enough, we can chuck the crappy things. How's your pitching arm?"

From his position among the clump of thistles on the crest, Revell could see the rest of his squad scattered

26

about the slope below him. From behind, at the bottom of the reverse slope, came the constant throbbing of the Chinook's engines. He'd kept Cohen with him, and maintained radio contact with the pilot. They might need a fast getaway soon.

"Any sign of that ECM aircraft yet?"

"Still on our own at the moment, Major."

"OK, let me know the moment it's on station." Hell, they were on their own alright. A full major, and his command consisted of six men, seven if he counted Kurt—and he wished he didn't have to—and Andrea.

Another week and he'd have been putting together his new Special Combat Company, but this had come along first, a task more suited to a regiment than a squad. The rain was easing at last, that was something.

Away to his right he could see Sergeant Hyde, his face locked to the tripod-mounted Hughes sight-and-command box. Black threads of cable snaked from it in all directions, to the various launchers and missiles scattered across the ground between them and the road. Kurt lounged beside the sergeant, smoking, with one arm draped nonchalantly over an M60 machine gun.

Libby was off to the major's left, manning the command box for the decoys, and down the slope from him were Clarence and the girl. Andrea had her favourite M16, with a grenade launcher clipped under the barrel. Through his binoculars, Revell could see her jacket pulling in at the waist and stretching tight over the backside it didn't quite cover. Yes, she was quite something. He'd not told

27

the colonel of his suspicions about her being the one who'd incinerated the Russian prisoner; though if he was honest with himself, he knew that they were more than suspicions. Lippincott would have privately applauded the action, but for the sake of appearances he'd have been forced to hook her out, and into a POW camp.

He couldn't help himself, Revell was fascinated by her. Not just because she was so incredibly beautiful, not even because her aura of hardness made her such a challenge; it was something else, something much deeper. Maybe it was a reflection of a submerged facet of his own make-up. If they ever should make love, however willingly she did it, he could imagine it being a fight. His body confirmed what his mind wouldn't admit—the prospect excited him.

That bitch of an ex-wife of his had never been prepared to explore new ways of making love. How many times had he offered to do anything she wanted? It must have been hundreds, and she'd called him a pervert. There had been a time, in the early days of the marriage, when he'd have happily been the bitch's slave, done anything to please her, but all she'd ever wanted, and he'd suspected not even really wanted, was sex rarely, quickly and cleanly.

She'd always kept a box of Kleenex by the bed, and almost before he'd withdrawn she'd thrust a handful at him, telling him to "wipe yourself, you're dripping on the quilt." Seconds later she'd cork herself with more of the same and disappear into the bathroom for half an hour.

It was no more than wishful thinking, but he could

imagine it being very different with Andrea . . .

There was another dull boom followed by a ripple of minor explosions, closer this time. The Russians were clearing another pattern of mines. He had perhaps five more minutes to himself. It seemed that it was only in the last moments before an action, when everything had been done and checked and all there was to do was wait, that he ever really got the chance to spend a few minutes exploring his own thoughts.

His gaze flickered to the mortar, and Dooley and Burke. An unlikely pair: Dooley, the big mercurial scrounger from New York, and Burke, the oldest member of the squad, from an unfashionable part of London, who had a complaint for every occasion and an excuse for avoiding work just as often. Still they got on well enough. Pity the whole of NATO couldn't manage such harmony. If they could, then weapon standardisation would be progressing faster, and the M60s might get changed for the excellent British light support weapon.

Again he saw Andrea. She'd shifted position slightly, bending one leg so that the material of her camouflage suit was pulled tight into her backside. What sort of underwear would she have on, if any? Hell, she was turning into an obsession, he was concentrating on the wrong things . . . but he felt he was right, about her putting up a fight to add spice to intercourse. He'd not mind getting hurt, not if she did it; it'd be worth it, perhaps he'd enjoy the pain. There had been one occasion, years ago, before he was married, when he'd run a girlfriend's mother to

29

the airport . . .

He'd always thought Karen's mother attractive, had indulged in an occasional fantasy when a long petting session with Karen had got him worked up, and he'd had to relieve the throbbing pain of frustration on getting back to his room. Heck, he'd always felt guilty about it. She must have been at least twice his age, getting on for forty, and anyway, you don't think that sort of thing about your girlfriend's mother . . . besides, it was Karen's fault for not letting him go all the way.

It was his first decent car, and he was proud of it, had paid for it himself, well *was* paying for it, gradually. They'd started out early, and they'd had lots of time in hand.

Perhaps it was her maturity, she never giggled or sulked; or maybe it was her looks, her make-up was always perfect and her figure impressive. That day she'd been wearing a T-shirt and tight jeans. His eyes had kept straying to the front of her jutting top.

"You like my new shirt?" she'd asked.

He'd plunged, and known he'd blush as he did. "I like what's in it."

Christ, in the long twenty seconds after that he'd gone through agonies while she'd fixed him with a look he couldn't comprehend. The breath she'd taken had only made his eyes stray more.

"Pull over here." Her voice had sounded different, huskier.

There had been no need to park right in among the trees, but he had. If she was going to make a scene he didn't want anyone seeing, not until he'd had a chance to say sorry, cool her down.

"That was naughty of you. Don't you think I should punish you, or do you think you should punish me, for not being angry?"

Her hand was in his lap, kneading his erection. Shit, at that moment he'd have swopped the flashy red coupe for any clunker that had a bench front seat.

The way they clambered into the back, the clumsy tangling of arms and legs, were all a merciful blur. The next clear image was the soft white breast being crushed into his face, a hard pink nipple pressing against his lips until it gained entry, when he had to gasp for breath. And all the time she'd whispered, "You can hurt me, you can hurt me." Then the frantic contortions to reach buttons and fasteners, and she'd come before he was ready, clutching painfully hard at his body. Nails had raked his back and thighs. He'd slipped out, been unable to re-enter, and had finished on her smooth warm belly, ignoring the biting soreness as he rubbed against her body hair.

He'd broken up with Karen soon afterwards, and they'd moved that summer. The bruises had faded, but the deep scratches took longer to heal and he'd often examined them in the mirror. There had not been a second time, though he'd tried to make opportunities, driven past often enough . . .

The T84 driving cautiously into view looked squat, ugly and powerful. A second followed several lengths behind, and then a third. Revell lifted his respirator from where it hung about his neck, and used its built-in short range radio.

"OK everyone, take it easy. This is just the advance guard, we're waiting for the main body." He saw the lead tank stop a good way short of the last lot of mines they had scattered. "Meanwhile, let's see how they deal with that little problem."

"Same way as the others." Dooley's voice was easily recognisable on the radio. "Too fucking fast for comfort."

"Shut the yakking, just listen."

Hyde had been quick off the mark, getting in before Revell. That was why the major wanted him in the outfit. The hideously disfigured British NCO might resent having been drafted into the American squad, but he never let that interfere with his combat efficiency. When it came to tank busting, he was one of the best.

His record said nineteen Soviet tanks destroyed. It was possible that unconfirmed kills doubled that, and when an estimated number of APCs, armoured cars and ammunition trucks was added on, it made for one hell of an impressive total. Men like that were more precious than gold to their commanders, and no CO in his right mind was ever going to let one go. Well he'd got Hyde for a one-off special mission, and he was going to hang on to him, whether the sergeant liked it or not.

"Now what the hell is that?" Cohen parted the nettles for a clearer view of the strange vehicle motoring past the tanks. It halted a hundred yards from the highly visible mines.

"I think it's the reason for Dooley's discomfort."

For a moment the radio-man's question had echoed one in Revell's mind, then he examined the new-comer through his binoculars. It looked for all the world like an armoured fueller on tracks. A suspicion began to form.

Thick white vapour was hosed at tremendous pressure from a small remote controlled turret, set above the heavily protected cab. The artificial cloud swept forward over the mines, feathering in the light wind. There was a distant "crack," as a flare bobbed from a discharger set into the turret front beside the stubby tube of the projector, and the dense floating mist became a roaring wall of yellow flame.

Instantly, there was a swift succession of explosions as every mine was triggered by the massive over-pressure. A pulsing wave of compressed and super-heated air raced outward, setting the meadow into wave-like motion.

It gave the major no satisfaction to have his guess confirmed. The clearance technique was a refinement of the aerosol bomb, an American invented fuel/air munition that was seeing wider and wider application, as commanders grew to fully appreciate its value as an area weapon, rather than just as a sledgehammer way of clearing mines and booby traps.

Before the mass of debris raised by the blast had settled, the tanks were moving again. It was self-preservation as much as discipline that prompted the crews to maintain a safe distance between each other. The mine clearer began to follow, as the first vehicle of the column's main body came into sight.

"They're not bunching. They're going to motor

straight through." Hyde's fingers hovered over the miniature keyboard. What was that bugger waiting for? If Revell didn't give the order soon, at the rate the Ruskies were motoring they'd all be clear in another couple of minutes.

The slight cratering caused by the multiple detonations didn't even slow the T84s. They took it at speed, their suspensions soaking up the bumps and passing little of the jarring of the corrugations to their hulls.

"Make a hole in the road. Take out that fourth vehicle."

An anti-tank missile had jumped from the grass and was jetting toward its target even as Revell's order came through. Hyde only had to keep the sight aligned on the target, as the flame-tailed projectile skimmed the tops of the grass, receiving its commands from the control box via the twin wires unreeling behind it.

Struck as it traversed the broken section, the round's powerful warhead punching effortlessly through the side armour and into the pressurised fuel compartment, the Soviet mine clearer turned into a tracked bomb.

Ten times greater than its predecessor, the explosion sent flame, chunks of road and anonymous pieces of armour plate high into the air. A four-barrelled Shilka anti-aircraft tank, following fifty yards behind, was pushed off the road by the blast, and shed a track.

"OK, fire as targets present." They'd have to be quick now, hit and run. That second blast had flattened much of the meadow, making them conspicuous. Revell watched the crew of the flak-tank as they bailed out. The last man from the big radar-topped turret threw up his arms and tumbled over the side, as a third burst from Kurt found him.

Now the fields on either side of the road swarmed with targets, as the Russian column split up and drove around the obstructing crater. Hyde wasn't confused by the choice of victims. Playing the control panel like a concert pianist, he sent missile after missile toward the racing Soviet armour. His second round was also a hit, square on the skirt armour of a T84, but it kept going. There was no mistake with the third, it struck an exhaust-spewing T84, setting off its ammunition and sending its turret soaring into the air, accompanied by the flaming bodies of its crew.

"Ten rounds with the mortar, and then we get out." The chorus of protest from Hyde, Andrea and Clarence was not unexpected, but Revell knew it was too good to last—and it was.

It was Cohen who spotted the danger first. "There's a Shilka and a self-propelled gun looking like they mean business."

Using a disabled tank as cover, the quad-barrelled flak-wagon employed short bursts of tracer to direct the 152mm howitzer of the SP mount.

"Let them have the decoys." Sods of earth rained about them, as a high explosive shell struck the ground between Revell's and Hyde's positions. The major spat dirt and grass, holding his breath against the rasping fumes and stench of high explosive.

Well away from the crest, the fringe of a clump of trees was brightened by flashes, simulating the back-blast signature of rocket launchers. Other pyro-technique devices sent showers of powdered metal and foil strips into the air.

It worked. The flak-tank switched its fire. Blurs of red and white tracer laced the trunks, bursting with bright splashes on impact.

Unable to resist the broadside target presented by the self-propelled gun, as it slewed round to face its thickest armour toward the trees, Hyde fired his two remote Dragon rocket launchers at it simultaneously. Both rounds struck at the same moment and every road wheel and track link was blasted from the vehicle, and its engine torn out.

A last air-burst from the mortar banged off above the stricken SP gun, as a blackened figure struggled to escape from a roof hatch.

The range was too great for the 40mm grenades Andrea was firing to be effective, and she gripped the weapon tighter as successive rounds fell short. Beside her, Clarence fired carefully aimed single shots, bringing down two crewmen who had abandoned their T72 when its auxiliary fuel tanks had been opened and ignited by an air-burst, and now flared and spouted fire over the tank's rear.

It was time to get out, and Libby didn't need to be told. He was already pulling the leads from the box as the order came through. Kurt fired off the last of a belt and then both of them were up and running for the Chinook.

"Did you see that?" Dooley fell in step alongside them. "Put that last one down on the fucker's head, and I set off the spare gas on another. Not bad, eh?" He carried the mortar and two unused cases of bombs as though they were nothing. "Better than piddling about with a box of shitty gimmicks and fireworks, ain't it?"

The dig didn't bother Libby. He just did his job, whatever job he was given. For him the war didn't matter, staying in the Zone did. Blast it, that column had been slowed by no more than a few minutes. Now they'd be chasing off to get in front of it again, all the time getting nearer the edge of the Zone. That wasn't what he wanted. If he was going to find Helga he had to stay in, for as long as it took, if it took forever.

Clarence and Andrea were the last over the crest, and as they half-ran, half-skidded down to the helicopter, it erupted behind them under the savage pounding of several large calibre guns. They scrambled aboard as the Chinook's undercarriage lifted clear, and it skimmed away between the low hills, using them as cover until it was well beyond the range of the column's SAMs.

"See you got your stripes a bit dirty at last then." Burke added his grubby fingerprints to the smudges of mud despoiling the chevrons.

"Don't tell him that." Sensing entertainment, Dooley joined in. "Next thing you know he'll have us licking them clean for him."

"Not on your bloody life. Not for all the money and the other stuff he's got crammed in that flak-jacket."

It wasn't difficult for the corporal to ignore Burke. Now that they were flying again, it took all his concentration to stop himself from throwing up. Dear God, and he'd thought skimmers were bad, but those armoured hovercraft were nothing compared to the yo-yo flight pattern this mobile sex shop was executing.

"Oh, I don't know." Dooley had been considering the proposal. "If he threw in all his back pay. I know he hasn't spent any of his own money in the last year."

"He doesn't have to the way he wins at cards . . ."

"Sergeant Hyde has work for you two." Ignoring the ritual undertone of complaint and the pair's sour expressions, Revell sat down beside the communication board. "We know what road they're taking now. That advance guard took the left fork, so it's Frankfurt for certain. Pass. that on to our ECM merchant when it arrives. Is there any sign of it yet?"

"It'll be on station in a couple of minutes. Word is, it's a four-seat Prowler, so there's no way those Ruskies are going to yell for help, or chat to each other."

"Good. It's a pity they don't carry radar homing missiles. Could have taken out a flak-tank or two for us. Did you get that count I wanted?"

"Close as I could. I might have missed one, what with the smoke and filth they kept shovelling over us, but I figure we destroyed a couple of T84s, damaged two more and totalled a self-propelled gun. With that Shilka losing a track and Sergeant Hyde plastering the countryside with that fancy mine clearer, I reckon it's not a bad score."

Dooley staggered past, holding a crate whose other end he believed Burke to be supporting. "Chewed

38

them up real good, heh, Major?"

"Give him the other figure." Revell watched Dooley's face as Cohen referred to his message pad.

"Thirty-four, maybe thirty-five pieces of armour got past us. So you should chew a little harder next time."

"Do we have another go, or is that us finished? I'd like to know, I've got this vested interest—me."

"Yes, Dooley, we're having another go, and another, and another. Until we've slowed them enough to give our armour time to get into position for an interception, or until there's no more for us to have a go at."

"Or no more of us to have a go." Clarence had been listening to the major. There wasn't any fear in the sniper's voice, or doubt, or relish. He was simply making a statement.

If the sniper was expecting a snap denial then Revell would disappoint him. He nodded, "Or until there's no more of us left."

CHAPTER THREE

Burke threw the half-eaten slice of garlic sausage out of a window, and tried to wash away the taste with a gulp of Dooley's equally ferocious black coffee. He pulled a face as he returned the flask. "Bloody hell, what do you have for your ruddy afters, a bowl of pepper?"

"I like my food to have a bit of flavour. You don't know good food when you taste it." Using his bayonet, Dooley cut off a large chunk of the fat-marbled meat and popped it into his mouth. He chewed slowly, rubbing his belly in exaggerated enjoyment.

"Will you go and eat elsewhere!" Cohen's complexion was flickering through the spectrum again.

"If you ate some of this," Dooley illustrated his point by waving the powerful smelling sausage under the radio-operator's nose, "you wouldn't have all this silly fucking trouble."

"What are you offering him, kill or cure?"

Sergeant Hyde butted in. "Finish that muck fast or throw it out. The whole damned cabin stinks."

Major Revell was only half-aware of the conversation and exchanges going on behind him. They were back over the road again, and he was watching it from between the two pilots, looking for a natural obstacle that would stop the column and force it to deploy when they next brought it under fire. Too near the advancing Russians and there wouldn't be time to set it up; too far ahead and there would be no chance of setting up a third ambush if it were needed.

Hell, who was he kidding? Of course it would be needed. The way the Reds had ploughed past the first roadblock was proof of more than blind determination. He'd seen them come on like that before, lots of times, and later interrogation had always uncovered the nature of the orders that had driven them suicidally on. The words "or else" were never actually included in the orders, but every Russian officer developed a genius for reading between the lines. False economy, particularly in respect of casualties, was never a factor behind the decisions arrived at by the Soviet Command. If a target was of sufficient importance, then forty tanks and two hundred and fifty men were utterly expendable to capture or destroy it.

Frankfurt was that important. The column, while formidable on any battlefield, was totally inadequate for taking a city, but the panic their appearance on the streets would cause, before they could be mopped up, would be catastrophic.

"That's what we want. Put us down there."

The chopper sank to a fast bouncy landing in a

42

field not far from the stone bridge. Revell had the door open before it settled, and was shouting instructions even as he jumped out.

"Cohen, get us air-support. Tell them we'll have a backed-up armoured column for them in . . . in forty minutes. Sergeant, I want explosives under that bridge, enough to bring down most of the span. Any mines we have left go on the far bank. Concentrate them at the most likely locations armour might use to cross."

"What about the bus?" The pilot had come out of the Chinook, and approached Revell as he assisted in the unloading of the stores.

"Hang on here until we're finished, then you can lift us to that farm over there." Revell indicated an extensive sprawl of barns and sheds, surrounding a shuttered four-story house fifteen hundred yards away.

"That's fine by me, just don't leave it too late. If we're in the air when the Ruskies show, then we won't be for long." He turned to go back in, then paused. "You need any help?"

"Every bit we can get. Take these over to the bridge."

"OK." The pilot held out his arms and accepted the load of explosives and fuses. "Matter of fact, I'll be glad when the last of this ordinance is off my old bus. Since I came over, I've mostly been hauling vehicle spares, it was beginning to get kinda boring. Now I reckon I'm looking forward to the stink of axle grease again."

The co-pilot was not as pleased to be roped in to help with the portering. The sweat that poured from

43

him, as he lugged the charges to where Libby was setting them against the underside of the single arch, had little to do with the effort involved. His peace of mind wasn't helped by Dooley who, seeing his nervousness, cut a thin slice from a block of plastic explosive and put a match to it right in front of him.

"Save the party tricks and get on with it," was the only rebuke offered by Hyde, as the co-pilot made a peculiar strangled noise and backed away, to turn and run clutching the seat of his pants to the nearest ditch.

Libby had rested the charges on the ledges of large steel 'I' beams, that had been set into the structure some time in the past to strengthen it. "That's the best I can do without more time to play around."

"That'll do." Revell looked over the parapet. "They're not going to see them, and even if they do it doesn't matter. Either way we slow them down, and they'll eventually be forced to make a wet crossing and then we get a real crack at them."

"I don't think we'll be getting many of them with these." Hyde tapped his foot against a collection of mines, most of them small anti-personnel types. "Even using them in pairs, they're unlikely to break a track on a T84."

"Set them anyway. We may get lucky, and they'll catch any infantry they send to check the banks."

"Trucks coming, Major." It was Burke who saw the approaching convoy first.

"What in hell's name is going on? The MPs have had enough time to stop all the traffic. How come half a dozen six-wheelers have slipped through?" Revell walked out into the middle of the road.

"Clarence, take Kurt and flag them down. Tell them to turn around and get their arses out of here."

Although he'd said nothing to her, Andrea inevitably tagged along with the sniper. She ignored Kurt's leer. An afterthought struck the major. It was a long shot, but worth a try. He called out after the trio.

"Check what loads they're carrying."

At only fifteen yards wide, Revell wasn't sure that the water flowing between the steep banks could really be graced with the title of river. It sure wasn't the Rhine, but the recent rain had raised its level appreciably, as the flattened weeds along the bank showed. He could only guess at its depth, but it certainly wasn't more than six feet at best. But that would be enough.

The Russian armoured personnel carriers were amphibious, but the tanks weren't. They would either have to waste time preparing for deep wading, or find another bridge or ford. The delay might be long enough for an airstrike to be effective. Spaced out along the road and moving fast the column was a difficult target, it would be a different matter if they could be caught waiting to cross. Andrea was suddenly beside him.

"There is something you should see."

It was the first time she had spoken to him directly in three days. As usual, her tone and expression were neutral. He followed her to the trucks, wishing that she was wearing the tight jeans in which he'd first seen her.

"It's mostly PX stores, Major." Clarence waved his hand over the line. "There's even a mobile library, but I thought the one at the end might be of interest."

45

When Revell walked down the line, at first glance the last vehicle in the convoy looked no different from any of the others. He couldn't see what the sniper was getting at. Its cargo area carried only an assortment of roped-down packing cases containing gun spares. Then he saw the two-wheel trailer on the back, and identified the lettering on its container.

"I think we just hit pay dirt." He called out to the driver. "Is this ALX in here?"

"Ain't it just. I pulled the short straw and had to hitch it to my rig. Why do you think I'm tail end Charlie of this bunch?"

"Drive it over to the far side of the bridge. The Sergeant will show you where he wants it."

At Revell's words the driver switched off his engine and leapt from his cab. "Hey, I ain't no combat soldier, I'm a truck driver. I reckon I've been shit on enough by having to tow a trailerful of liquid explosive all the way out here, I'll be damned if I'm going to start messing about with the goop." The driver turned his attention to the other members of the convoy. All five vehicles were executing lumbering three-point turns on the narrow road. His full attention snapped back to the major when he saw the Colt being pointed in his direction.

"I've neither the time nor the patience to argue. Get in, start up, and drive . . ."

"You can't do that . . ."

". . . where I told you. Now." Thrusting the barrel to within an inch of the driver's chin, Revell looked him straight in the eye. "I said now." He cocked the .45. "Soon as we've used that part of your load you can be off."

46

"Alright, I'm doing it, see I'm doing it." Without further prompting the driver boarded again and, the minute the other trucks had completed their turns and were out of the way, drove across the bridge.

By the time Revell was back on the bridge, Hyde and Dooley had started to spray the liquid explosive on to the far bank. It soaked into the earth immediately, leaving no trace. The largest concentration was used two hundred yards downstream, where turbulence beneath the river's surface indicated a shallower stretch, and thus a possible fording place. Libby put one of the anti-personnel mines into the centre of each treated patch, to act as a trigger.

"And when this is done, do we go and hide, like the last time?" Cradling her M16, Andrea watched the work in progress.

"What would you like us to do, strap grenades to our bodies and chuck ourselves under their tracks?" It irritated Revell that, in every one of their brief exchanges, he was invariably forced on to the defensive. "We'll use what resources we've got the best way I know how. Now get back to the chopper, we're almost through." The way she always kept him at a distance just had to be deliberate. Not that he'd ever said anything, made any obvious move; but she instinctively sensed his interest, and was wary, avoided giving him encouragement.

The riverbank had now been treated for a considerable distance on either side of the bridge, and with the last drop of ALX used up, the truck was wallowing back on to the road. Without any sign or acknowledgement from the driver it sped off back the way it had come, not waiting for all the equipment to

47

be stowed away, dragging the hose and injection device behind it.

Apart from the tracks in the grass, barely visible even at close quarters, there was no sign of the treatment they had given the area. Revell felt the increased draught from the Chinook's blades as the pilot anticipated the order to pull out.

It was barely an hour since they'd left the site of the first ambush. Soon the Russian column would be here, and the process would begin all over again. And how many more times after that? The orders said to harass and delay the column. Why in hell's name didn't he admit, at least to himself—he had no intention of obeying those orders? He wasn't going to use the lives of his men just to buy a few minutes. No, he wasn't about to harass the Soviet armour, he was about to destroy it.

"Suit up. There may be some residual muck down there." Revell unrolled his NBC suit and began to put it on. It wasn't easy to keep balance in the hovering craft, and he constantly had to grab at a bulkhead for support as he pulled on the leggings.

Until they were right over it, the deserted farm had looked much the same as any other. It was Kurt whose sharp eye for detail had noticed the two-yard diameter dead patches in the surrounding fields, and among the weeds infesting the lanes and courtyards.

The pilot set them down on the drive leading to the sprawling house, and the moment they'd unloaded their equipment, made off at speed to find a safe place to await their recall.

48

A Volvo estate stood rusting on deflated tyres in front of the house, its tailgate up, a storm-toppled pile of mouldering cases nearby.

"Must have been a long time ago." Hyde completed his sampling checks of the air and soil. "There's enough residual muck around the impact points to keep the plants down, but no harm to us. Not unless we start eating dirt."

"Not much chance of that." Burke broke off pieces of dead rosebush from the border below the windows. "Mind you, smother it in sauerkraut and Dooley would probably try it." He toed a fragment of shell casing into a shallow crater beside the door. Elsewhere the chemical rounds had done virtually no damage, beyond a hole in a barn roof and cracked windows in a nearby greenhouse.

"Don't waste any of this shit by letting it bury itself, do they? Must use some sort of retarding device before impact." Cohen turned over what might have been part of a miniature air-brake in his gloved hand.

"I wouldn't know, and I can't say I care." Dooley joined the others in pulling his respirator off. He sniffed the air cautiously. "When this crap comes flying down I don't stand about making fucking notes. I usually try for a new standing start speed record." The first attempt he made to push the partially open front door had met with resistance. He gave a second, harder, shove.

There was a body just inside, or what was left of one. Severely decomposed where it had been exposed to what weather had found its way in, the still recognisable remains bore the marks of scavenging rats and foxes. A bunch of keys lay among the scattered bones of a hand, and false teeth glared glossy bright in the face of a hollow-eyed skull.

They entered one at a time, skirting the remains, save for Kurt who slothered through them, kicking bones and scraps of cloth and tissue across the floor.

"Right, we'll set up in a second-floor front room." Revell didn't bother to investigate any of the rooms leading off the lobby. "Cohen, I want you to stay on that radio until you get me air support or the damned thing melts. Dooley and Burke can plant the missiles among those outbuildings beside the big barn. I want the cables run back to the house. Let's move."

"I'm going to keep away from you." Burke waited for Dooley to pick up two of the heavy missiles, before choosing one for himself. "People are beginning to think I'm musclebound as well. Wait for me, then . . ."

The house was fully furnished, and the curtains and carpets gave off a musty smell and clouds of dust at each disturbance. There were piles of leaves in every corner, and more rustled underfoot on the bottom stairs. Kurt threw open every door they passed, bringing violent sound to a house that had known none since the last shell of the gas barrage.

A large bedroom provided precisely the aspect required, and while Hyde set up the weapon control box on a dressing table by the window, Cohen produced a huge cloud of dust when he dragged aside a duvet and set the radio on the bed.

It was stupid really, Clarence admitted that to himself as he wandered along the corridor, looking into every room. He could have done it anywhere, who would ever know, or object. When he did find what was obviously the toilet he hesitated, and out of habit almost knocked before walking in, to a shock that stopped him dead.

There was a long pause before he could take another faltering pace. The little figure kneeling crouched over the bowl looked so . . . so alive. Its pretty print dress had only faded a little, and long blonde hair still fell around a face he was so thankful he couldn't see. Alone in that room, the child had died and been perfectly preserved, mummified in the tinder-dry atmosphere.

Everything else forgotten he backed out, carefully and quietly closing the door. Kurt was outside, cramming watches and jewellery into various pockets. A look of interest and cunning came into his face as he misinterpreted the sniper's behaviour. He grabbed at the door handle, and a rifle butt smacked into the side of his head. Cannoning off the wall his knees began to buckle, until the barrel of Clarence's Enfield jammed into his Adam's-apple and forced him to remain upright.

"One step in there and I'll kill you." He rammed the rifle harder into Kurt's throat. "Now get lost, understand? *Verstehen?*" Easing the pressure he allowed the Grepo to wriggle free, then prodded him away down the corridor.

As his brain began to recover from the effects of the blow, it momentarily looked as if Kurt might be harbouring thoughts of retaliation, but the sniper's eyes were still on him. He hesitated briefly, then wiped the blood trickling from the cut above his ear

51

and went up to the top floor. His boots echoed on the narrow uncarpeted stairway.

More cautiously than before, Clarence investigated the other rooms. The third he tried held a tableau as poignant as the earlier one. On a rumpled bed sprawled the body of a young woman. Beside it, on the floor, lay a male corpse. Both were quite perfectly preserved. In one hand the man held the woman's trailing fingers, in the other the smashed remains of a tumbler. A fluffy sheepskin rug still outlined where the spilled water had run.

"The Russians have killed so many. What is it about these that you find . . . special?"

He didn't turn round at Andrea's voice. "Perhaps it's just that, that there isn't anything special about them. As you say, there have been so many . . ." The memories flooded back and Clarence tried to fight them down, force them back into the dim recesses of his mind. The good, distant, past was gone, lost; remembering it would be too painful. The bad, recent, past hurt too, but there was nothing to be gained by trying to forget that, when every day he saw it re-enacted over and over again, like here, now.

Libby heard the conversation, but hesitated before going in. They were a funny bloody pair. He'd got on alright with Clarence before the girl had appeared on the scene, nothing close, but closer than anyone else had ever got to the sniper. Still, at least Hyde no longer regarded him as the sniper's keeper—that had been a ruddy bind.

There were times when he could do with a bit of female companionship himself. Even on his last leave he'd managed to keep the promise he'd made to himself, not to have a woman until he found Helga, but it became more difficult each time he was tempted. Christ, he was only human.

He stuck his head around the door. "Been looking bloody everywhere for you two. The Reds are on their way." Libby saw the bodies. "Left it a bit late, didn't they? Major says he wants you in place now. Four launchers have been put in the stable block for you."

"Tell him we'll be along in a moment. We're only close-in defence, he can start the killing without us. We'll catch up."

CHAPTER FOUR

Hyde's right hand moved to the control box and rested lightly on it as the head of the column came into range. The last of the cables from the remotely positioned missiles had been plugged in, and he was all set. It wouldn't be quite yet though, first he'd wait and see the effect of the charges beneath the bridge, and the mines and ALX. He dimmed the bright daylight display on the screen and pressed his face into the hood, into his own private world.

The magnified image was only an inch in front of his eyes. He panned along the spaced-out column and made careful adjustments to the focus, until the lead tank showed up with perfect clarity. Now it was just him and it. Strange how he always thought of tanks as living things, almost forgetting their crews. Perhaps it had something to do with the way they reacted to the impact of the powerful warheads he sent at them.

Some died instantly, grinding to a halt with smoke and flame pouring from them. Others went more quietly, slowing to a gentle stop, main guns drooping. And for a few there was another, rarer way.

Like huge stricken animals they'd go crazy, moving erratically, lurching and shuddering, even ramming others of their own kind. Sometimes he would fire a second missile to finish them off.

His total score was about thirty-nine. Whether they were confirmed or not didn't matter to him; he knew. Out of those, he'd only seen the crews on perhaps six or seven occasions, and then they had appeared no more than parasites leaving a dying host.

Shifting the nagging weight of the flak-jacket to a more comfortable position, Cohen jotted down the incoming message. "Major. I got some news. Which do you want first, the good or the bad?"

"Just give it to me straight. I haven't got the patience for party games."

"I just found us a pair of Thunderbolts. They've given me an ETA of fifteen minutes, but they've only got a part load, been diverted from another mission."

"What do they have?" Not that it made any difference, Revell knew that. They could find a use for whatever stores the ground attack aircraft were carrying. Anything that helped lower the odds was welcome, they were in no position to be fussy.

There was the inevitable consulting of the message pad. "Four pylons apiece, free fall stuff, an even mix of super-napalm and iron bombs; retarded thousand-pounders. And their drums are quarter-full, so they can give us a short storm of 30mm if we want it."

"Tell them they won't be taking any of it back home, and we'll call the targets as they make their final approach. And you'd better warn them these Ruskies aren't short of flak-wagons or SAMs."

Now the first tank was almost on the bridge. Revell's hand closed around the radio-control device and, at the very moment the T84 reached the centre of the span, crashed his thumb down hard.

The bridge disappeared inside a huge cloud of dust, spray and debris. Blocks of stone flew high into the air, towing streamers of smoke. As the rubble fell back, so the dust cloud cleared. One of the strengthening girders, twisted but still in place, was all that remained of the arch. The tank, its tracks gone, all of its road wheels buckled or missing, lay upside down in the river, barely visible among the turbulent water it partially dammed.

There were several near collisions as the rest of the vehicles turned off the road and deployed in the fields alongside. Revell watched through his binoculars. "Seems to be a discussion going on. Any minute now they'll send some poor devil to test the bank for mines and the water for depth. Hold your fire, we'll see what happens before we stir them up again."

A T72 had lowered the bulldozer blade beneath its hull front and was moving forward to tackle the riverbank, watched by dozens of figures who had appeared at the hatches of other vehicles. As the tank reached the river, the ground erupted benath it. With both tracks broken and uncurling on the meadow behind it, the T72 slid down into the water, until the flood reached the base of its turret. Hatches flew open and the turret crew baled out. For a moment it looked as if one of them was going to assist the driver, struggling to escape from his submerged compartment, but the tank slid in further and he didn't, joining the other crewmen in jumping on to dry land.

There was another explosion and two bodies were tossed high by the blast. The driver finally managed to free himself, crawled up on to the canted engine deck and crouched there, too terrified to step off.

"Looks like it's a bloody stalemate, don't it?" Careful not to disturb the sergeant's equipment, Burke set the machine gun at the window. "They move and the mines get them. We open up and they get us."

"Fuck off you miserable bastard." Dooley brought in three cases of ammunition. "Can't you ever think of anything cheerful to say?"

"How about getting out of here, before the commies do a demolition job on this place with us still inside?"

"I can see movement down by the bank. I think they've . . ." Hyde didn't finish the sentence. Another tall fountain of mud, water and weeds erupted as a legless torso cartwheeled into the river.

"They've got infantry down there, clearing a way." Revell looked at his watch. "Where the hell are those planes?"

"Coming in from the west now, right on the ground." Cohen carried the communication pack by its straps to the window. "They've got us in sight, and want to know where to lay their eggs."

"Tell them to beat up the far bank, both sides of the bridge, but save the heavy stuff this time round."

The Thunderbolts came in side by side at treetop

58

height, and on their first pass cut a bloody swathe through the Russian infantry. Panicking survivors and the deluge of high velocity shells set off more of the mines and caused further casualties.

Revell spotted a group of Russian vehicles more closely spaced than the rest and, in answer to the aircrafts' request for further targets, ordered Cohen to pass the information on.

Barely twenty seconds later they reappeared from another direction, but the column's anti-aircraft defences were ready this time. Tracer of every calibre and colour hosed upward, and from a missile carrier came the stabling flare of flame tails, as SAMs hurled themselves after the camouflage-painted planes.

Decoy flares rippled from the Thunderbolts as they screamed over the collection of Russian armour, their titanium plated bellies shrugging aside the hail of machine gun and radar directed 23mm cannon fire. Four long slim finned bombs littered the sky after their passing, each deploying a miniature parachute.

The drogues slowed the bombs' falls, allowing the jets to escape before the earth was rocked by four monstrous explosions. A 122mm self-propelled gun tipped on its side, and was part-buried under a shower of steaming earth. An APC was torn apart by a near miss that scattered flaming debris around a giant crater, and another simply ceased to exist as it took the full force of a direct hit. The last victim of the bombs was the missile carrier. Its radar torn away, the side of its hull crushed in, it began to burn.

Skimming the ground, the Thunderbolt pilots used every tree, every fold in the terrain to aid their getaway. They had almost made it when there was a vivid yellow flash from the leader's port engine tailpipe.

"He's hit." Cohen watched as the aircraft shed fragments of panelling and, towing a streamer of unburnt fuel, dipped to almost touch the ground.

"He'll make it." The sight of both aircraft, still in formation, hopping over a far hilltop added weight to Hyde's prediction. "I've seen those buggers flying with one engine shot away and half a wing gone."

"Better get ready, Sergeant." It wasn't immediately clear to Revell precisely what the Russians were intending to do, as every piece of amphibious armour began to roll forward. Then, when every weapon aboard them opened up on the bank, he understood.

The last of the mines was detonated by the barrage, and the APCs surged ahead, each choosing its own crossing point.

"Hit them as they climb out."

That was the order Hyde had been waiting for. The banks were steep and slippery, and the personnel carriers were soon in trouble, all of them having difficulty in hauling themselves from the river. The first one to succeed took long enough for Hyde to put a precisely guided rocket into its exposed and highly vulnerable thin belly armour.

The front mounted engine bore the brunt of the powerful charge, and as the vehicle slid back into the water, burning fuel gushed from its buckled hull, withering the rain-soaked weeds and briefly swirling on the fast current. It began to founder immediately and, as wounded infantry tried to hoist themselves through opened roof hatches, turned turtle and sank,

60

forming a second obstruction to the flow.

Even as Hyde aligned on another tempting target, the farmhouse shook to a giant hammer blow, and the room was filled with dust as the door was torn from its hinges and the windows blew out.

"Where the sodding hell did that come from?" Snorting to clear dust from his nostrils, Burke picked himself up from the floor, then voluntarily consigned himself to it again as two more shells plunged into the paved area fronting the house.

Slabs of concrete and masses of gravel pounded and peppered the farmhouse, smashing every last pane.

"I've got them." Swivelling the command box, Hyde brought it to bear on the T84 and pair of APCs that were fast closing in on them. His index finger stabbed down, and nothing happened. He got the same result from the other buttons he tried. "They've got the cables."

Supported by fire from a battery of self-propelled guns on the far side of the river, the infantry vehicles and their attendant tank were still coming on. The T84 opened up, its stabilised gun staying locked on target as the hull followed the undulations of collapsed field drains. A two-storey wing was struck by the shell, and had most of its roof lifted off by an explosion that filled its windows with flame. At eight hundred yards the APCs joined in, rounds from their 73mm main guns punching into the outbuildings. A large greenhouse dissolved in a cascade of shining shards as a shell detonated inside.

Kurt and Libby tumbled into the room. They were white with powdered plaster and their NBC suits

61

were scorched and slashed. The German was swearing passionately and incomprehensibly as he ex-tracted a long sliver of lathing from his arm.

"One minute we were looking out of the attic," Libby had to pause to spit dust, "the next the ruddy floor had gone and we were coming down faster than we went up."

"We can't do any more here." Hyde began pulling the leads from the box. "Might be an idea to pull back while we still can. Once those battle taxis start dropping their passengers it won't take them long to cut us off. This place is pretty isolated."

The men were hanging on his next words, Revell knew that. In effect the decision had already been made for him. Their teeth had been drawn and now it was only sensible to get out while they could. A broad stretch of open farmland behind the house would have to be traversed before they made it to the comparative safety of distant woods. For a short while, the Russian infantry's preoccupation with the farm would give them that chance.

But he hated having to retreat, the job only half done. With the remaining ten missiles they might have inflicted sufficient damage to force the column to turn around. Instead, they had to be the ones to turn and run.

"Smash what we can't carry. We'll be moving fast." The major ducked instinctively as more shell fragments smacked into the house. A seat from the Volvo had come to rest on the window box, and hung precariously for a moment, filling the room with white smoke as it smouldered, before falling off to complete the journey the explosives had started it on.

"We'll pick up Clarence and Andrea on the way."

Five hundred yards away the tank had stopped, and was maintaining a steady fire in support of the APCs which were still coming on, making good use of their own armaments as they did.

The corridor and stairs were filled with the wreckage of smashed furniture, sagging plasterboard and broken beams. Debris cluttered most of the rooms they passed, but others were curiously untouched by the devastation, save for their broken windows.

A still-settling heap of rubble filled the porch, almost completely blocking the door. Accurate bursts of heavy machine gun fire raked the house front and ricocheted wildly from the surface of the drive in showers of gravel.

Revell found a downstairs window from which he could make a safe reconnaissance of the stable block where the couple had set up their post. Sparks flew thickly about it from a burning woodpile close by. There was no way out of the place that was not swept by the Russian automatic fire.

The troop carriers had slowed, but were still advancing; the couple would have to make their move soon. Receiving no acknowledgement of his urgent instructions to them, he put the respirator mask to his face again and repeated it. Clarence briefly appeared at a doorway, waved, and disappeared inside again.

Revell watched the seconds flickering by on his Omega. What the hell was keeping them? Would the sniper send her first, or would he make the run to test the dangers? It was fruitless to speculate. The miniature liquid crystal bars built and destroyed the seconds, telling him he would know soon enough.

Arriving in a flat trajectory at virtually point-blank range, the round fired by the T84 gave no warning of its approach. It scored a direct hit. The stable block fell apart, collapsing in a welter of shattered bricks and beams.

He wasn't conscious of any noise. To Revell's eyes it seemed the single-storey structure broke up in silent slow motion, first bulging outward as the shell exploded in its heart, then disintegrating as the roof that had been lifted off fell back and found no walls to support it. Only a half-buried saddle and horse-shoes nailed to jutting splintered rafters gave any clue as to what the mound of rubble might once have been.

"Bugger," Hyde had witnessed the destruction as well, "he was a bloody good sniper. Stupid way for him to go, after all he's been through. Pretty much the same way as his wife and kids."

It took an effort, but Revell fought down the urge to rush out and claw at the mound. It would serve no useful purpose to add his body to the ruin. He scrutinised the tank. There was nothing he could do now, but he would know it again. If the opportunity arose . . . and he'd make it . . . he'd extract a bloody revenge . . .

"Get them moving, Sergeant. Don't let them bunch."

Kurt was the one who set the pace as they ran toward the trees a good half a kilometre away. Behind them, the shelling and machine gunning roared to a crescendo as the APCs closed on their objective.

Hurdling a flooded ditch, Cohen slipped on landing and sprawled in the mud. Shit, he'd have to convert some of his haul into paper, the flak-jacket weighed him down like a lead suit and, added to the bulk of his NBC outfit, slowed him to half the others' speed.

Maybe he'd mail some of his loot back home, have Manny get a price for it next time he went into Chicago. And then again, maybe not. His brother-in-law was too full of good ideas, and too full of himself. Trust within a family is a fine thing, but at four thousand miles that was stretching trust just a little too far. And if Ruth saw the jewellery . . . once she tried it on, it'd be easier to cut out her heart while she was still breathing than to get her to part with it again. He'd better dispose of it himself. He'd get the best price he could when he was next in Koblenz or Bonn. So it was a buyer's market, better some than none.

"Come on, Corp, must be those new stripes slowing you down."

Cohen felt Dooley's huge hands clamping on his shoulders and dragging him to his feet. The moment's rest had done him good, his chest didn't hurt anymore.

"Shame about the girl. Waste of a nice arse." Dooley glanced back at the collection of buildings. It was surprising, apart from a little smoke and a few chunks out of the house, it hardly looked at all damaged. "You ready?"

"Why the concern?" Cohen set off at a jog.

Dooley took the radio-man's pack from him, added it to his own considerable load and kept pace alongside. "Don't you know? I'm your heir, I am. When you go down for keeps I'll be the first one along to pick up the pieces. The pieces that are worth money, that is. From now until your death rattle you have me for a buddy, every minute of every hour we're in action. What's up, don't you like the idea?"

"I should be grateful? A vulture for a friend I don't need. And about that death rattle. Don't hold your breath waiting for it. You should live so long as to make a profit out of this bloodsucking scheme."

"Yeah? Well I reckon I'll be collecting on the deal real soon. See, I'm gonna bill you every time I save your life, or carry your pack, or . . ."

A spurt of speed, a quick wrench and Cohen had retrieved the radio before Dooley could stop him. "You hanging about I can't help; you getting your hands on my money I can." Cohen patted one of his full pockets. "Break your heart, not my bank."

An "over" from the barrage going down around the farm dug a crater uncomfortably close to the two men, showering them with liquid soil, worms and soggy heads of wild corn. Both of them hunched lower, and conserved their breath for running.

Dooley was annoyed. Shit, what a tight-wad . . . but he had patience and the way the war was going, he wouldn't have to be patient for too long. The Zone saw a hell of a turnover in personnel, a shell could turn the little Yid over at any time. Just like one had that limey sniper and the German broad. Jesus what a waste that was . . . that beautiful arse, what a waste . . .

*   *   *

66

Clarence scrabbled at the collapsed masonry, not caring what injury he did his hands as he pushed and threw the rubble aside. He saw a movement, too regular to be settlement, crawled to the tangle of splintered roof beams and began to remove the mass of tiles they supported. An opening appeared, the last few shards slithered and crashed about him, and he was suddenly afraid to look inside the hole that had appeared.

The last time he had done that, what had looked back at him had been so horrible, so pitiful, and just recognisable as one of his own children. Then it had been a Russian bomber, now it was a shell, and Andrea, not his family; but he was still afraid of what he would see. Not daring to look, he turned his face to the sky and felt the light rain wash the dust from his skin.

There were so many hatreds in him, but the greatest and most passionate he aimed in that direction. "God's will" the priest had said, "suffer little children" . . . and he thought again of those ruined young bodies and his darling wife, and wished he'd not suppressed the temptation to smash the platitude-mouthing old fool in the face.

"Take this, take it."

The sniper saw the Viper rocket launcher being thrust out toward him. He stretched down and hauled the projector out of the way, then reached for her hand. It was bloody—missing two nails and the tip of the thumb.

Both the APCs and the tank were now concentrating their fire on the farmhouse, while the barrage from the supporting guns had shifted to the fields on either side. The shelling ceased abruptly as he pulled Andrea clear.

Her hands and face were flecked and streaked with blood, and a large livid bruise showed on her left cheek. She stood up, shook the dust from her hair, and Clarence knew she was alright. He reached toward her and pulled a cobweb from her hair. It was the first time he had ever touched her, almost their first physical contact of any kind. The undeclared barrier that existed between them came down again, Clarence triggering it by abruptly withdrawing his hand.

"They'll be coming in now. We need better cover, I'll go first." He meant to sprint, but every joint and muscle ached from the pounding his body had taken, forcing him to a slower pace. Machine gun bullets struck the ground about him, drilling holes in the corner of the house as he reached its sanctuary.

Andrea followed, losing precious seconds as she slipped on the loose piled bricks. She was halfway when the sharply raked frontal armour of the leading personnel carrier ploughed through the sagging remains of a tractorshed and into view.

Every crew-port on the vehicle was open, and from each projected the bullet-spitting barrel of the infantry's AKMs. The bullets chased Andrea as she threw herself down and rolled to a firing position, shouldering the rocket tube. Marching spurts of gravel and stone cut toward her as she took aim.

CHAPTER FIVE

Ignoring the bullets striking sparks from the stone about her, Andrea took careful aim and fired the rocket at the troop carrier's hull side.

Capable of defeating twelve inches of solid armour, the APC's thin plate provided hardly any resistance to the high velocity jet of molten explosive, unleashed by the rocket's impact and detonation immediately below the vehicle's turret, the commander's position.

As though it had struck a cliff face the APC stopped dead, and its rear doors flew open as a pillar of spiralling flame burst from the turret hatch.

Nerve-shredding screams came from the vehicle. Clarence could hear them clearly above the erratic crackling of ammunition cooking off. A figure staggered from the wreck, wreathed in hoops of flame. Levelling his rifle he brought the reeling Russian into his sights, and held his fire. The apparition collapsed and squirmed in the mud, vainly trying to defeat the rippling hell encasing it. A last arching contortion and it was still, only the guttering flame and ugly black smoke giving it movement.

Discarding the single shot rocket tube, Andrea ran to the cover of the house. "The other is close, I can hear it . . ."

Slinging his rifle, Clarence reached out to take her arm and propel her away, but instead suddenly ripped her M16 from her grasp and swung the butt at her head. As she half-ducked, half-stumbled aside, the crushing blow grazed past her and hit something soft and yielding.

The blow he had aimed at the apparition had stopped it, and now it stood stock still, the bone-exposing claws of its charred hands still extended toward Andrea. A desperate hooting noise compounded of agony and distress came from the sufferer, as he rocked on the burnt stumps of his ankles. Every stitch of clothing had been consumed by the flame that still played amongst hanging ribbons and lace-like pendants of sloughing flesh, and the white of exposed bone showed on the head and arms of the anti-tank rocket's victim.

This time Clarence didn't hesitate, bringing up the rifle to fire. Andrea's hand clamped hard on the barrel and forced it down.

"No, let him live while he can." She snatched the weapon back. "He has done it to others, let him feel what it is like."

An imploring talon reached out for the sniper and he fended it off with a sweeping blow. It was too much for the furnace-roasted limb and the forearm snapped off at the elbow, eliciting a shrill screech from the Russian.

Clarence retched, thinking for a moment that he was gonig to throw up. Frantically, he scraped the wrist of his suit against the wall to wipe away the adhering blood-dappled soot-stained tissue. This wasn't how he wanted to fight his war: he was a sniper, his war was clinically clean, precise, remote. It didn't involve contact with walking corpses, loathsome spectres that had no right to be alive. Death for him was always at a distance, only on that messy job in the Hanover salient had he ever seen, close to, the faces of the men he was killing. Even then the action had been so wild, so fast, that the faces had blurred and merged until he couldn't recall any individual one.

The burn victim took another tottering step forward, and before Andrea could move again to stop him Clarence unslung his rifle and pumped three fast shots into the sufferer's upper chest and face. Blackened flesh and shards of bone burst from the Russian under the devastating impact of the big dum-dum bullets. They instantly and thoroughly completed the work of destruction the fire had started. Pink foam bubbled from the scorched cavity where the bottom jaw had been. A remaining eye stared accusingly at Clarence, made grotesquely large by the shriveling of the skin about it, bulging out over the protruding splinters of cheekbone, restrained only by a fire-welded lid. Shooting from the hip, Clarence put a last round into the unseeing eye. That entire side of the cadaver's head ruptured and broke open, scattering lumps of white sponge and matted tufts of crisped hair. Andrea tugged at

71

his arm.

"We have little time . . ."

Beside them, the wall bulged and shed flakes of brick and mortar as a shell exploded inside the house.

Their escape route through the farmyard had been turned into an assault course. The deluge of high explosive had crudely dismantled and scattered the remains of tractors and harvesters, cluttering the area with razor sharp sheets of steel and blazing tyres. A row of silos spouted feed-pellets and fertiliser from irregular holes. Oil and fuel from split drums added another hazard. They passed between the dismembered components of a grain conveyer and then they were clear, racing across the pockmarked fields for the far trees.

As they ran and stumbled across the shell-churned ground the distinctive discordant sounds of a Soviet V6 diesel came to them, spurring them to greater effort. The engine note rose to a thundering bellow, accompanied by the grinding squeal of abused tracks. They were just half-way when bullets began scything the long grass beside them.

"Hold it." Revell had to shout to make himself heard to the others, who were already plunging into the dense undergrowth. He'd held back on reaching the fringe of the trees, waiting for Dooley and Cohen to catch up, now he hurriedly brought his binoculars into use.

"Damn it, I know they're there, I saw them." Again and again he quartered the ground where he'd seen the two figures go down. Only the regular stabs of

72

flame from the secondary turret armament of a troop carrier, partly concealed by the farm buildings, kept him searching after he'd otherwise have given up. The fact that the Ruskies were taking an interest in the same strip of pasture was all he needed to reassure himself that he could still trust his senses.

"How much smoke can we make?"

"Nothing like enough." Hyde too had seen the mud-plastered forms crouched in the shallow crater, and had anticipated the officer's question. "Just three 40mm grenades. Even if we put them down right on the button, with this breeze . . ." He didn't need to elaborate.

"Maybe they'll get fed up waiting, and piss off." Having failed to beg the use of the sergeant's binoculars, Dooley now hovered about the major.

"Somehow I don't think so. That load of Reds must be good and bloody sore at us by now. Looks like this bunch are staying behind to do a thorough job." He knew it was no more than a gesture, the weapon was useless at that range, but Burke set up the M60 anyway.

Having annoyed Dooley immensely by obtaining a loan of the glasses first, Libby examined the distant couple. "They're not moving."

"There's not much room for them to move, not without offering themselves as a target." There was no question of pulling out now, Revell knew that. Even when he'd felt certain Andrea and the sniper were dead, he'd been reluctant; now he was positive they were still alive, there was no way he was going to leave until he was sure she was safe. And all the time the rest of the enemy column would be bulldozing its way toward Frankfurt. In two hours it could be out of the Zone, and by spreading terror among the West German civilian population, be clogging every road and railway and airport with refugees. The hand to mouth logistical support for the NATO forces fighting south of the city would be cut to a trickle virtually immediately. Defeat, and a further extension of the Zone, would follow fast. "We'll wait for them to make a break, then we'll try to draw the APC's fire and give what cover we can."

"Sounds good in fucking theory," Dooley kept his voice down as he spoke to Cohen, "but unless those Reds are gonna be obliging enough to get out of their battle taxi and stroll our way, it ain't actually gonna amount to a whole lot. I'm as keen to save that broad's sweet fanny as the Major, and even that headcase limey sniper has his uses," Dooley glanced at Libby, watching for any reaction to that remark, finding none, "but I can't see what we can do, not with these pea-shooters." The M60 looked toy-like in his huge hand.

"What we could do with is a miracle." Taking a last look through the binoculars before passing them to Dooley, Libby could see the trapped pair attempting to leave the crater and being forced to duck back as the slight movement attracted machine gun fire.

"I think maybe we've got one." Without offering an explanation, Cohen picked up the radio and ran to dump it beside Revell. "Major, one of the Thunderbolts is still hanging about. He don't want to take no eggs home and wants to know where you'd like 'em laid."

"Tell him thanks; dead centre on the farm. Tell

him we've troops close-by."

The jet was in sight before the noise of its approach could be heard. It flashed across the fields toward the cluster of buildings, now partially hidden by drifting smoke. As it closed it lifted to roof-top height and, two hundred metres from its target, released an unpainted silver pod from each outer wing-pylon.

Tumbling end over end, the big elongated teardrop-shaped cannisters fell away from the air-craft and arced toward the farm. Their impact was invisible to the distant watchers, but the wall of yellow fire that rose beyond the house wasn't. To a man, they stood and waited, watching the giant bubble of flame as it grew to its full size and began to rise and turn boiling black at the edges.

Libby counted the seconds to himself . . . two, three . . . the "four" was only part formed in his mind when the moment came. The instant the fireball began to shrink it was suddenly transformed, becoming a searing white and doubling, tripling, to envelop the whole farm, as the miniature cylinders of oxygen within it released their pressurised contents simultaneously. House, barns, silos, everything disappeared within the all-devouring glaring mael-strom of white fire.

He'd seen it all, there was not a weapon that Libby had not witnessed in action, nuclear, conventional or chemical, but there was something overpoweringly awe-inspiring about super-napalm. Whenever it was used on the battlefield men would stand and watch, thanking God, or whatever they believed in, that this time it was not going down on them. How many times had he walked through the ashes of those on whom it had, and the ashes of how many men? A hundred, a thousand? He didn't know because there was never enough left to form even a rough estimate, just a crumbling fragment of bone here, a fused rifle mechanism there, and that would be all that was left of a section, a platoon, even a company.

For five long seconds the white fire hid the farm, then in a moment it was gone, and the smoke that replaced it swiftly rose into the low clouds, propelled by the colossal temperatures that had been generated. In that brief span of time the farm had been destroyed, utterly. Only one end of the house still stood, and that at an angle, as though impatient to join its fellows heaped below it. The big sheets of metal cladding had been stripped from the barns and the surviving skeletal frames were buckled and glowing. A remaining silo dipped suddenly and its flame-scorched metal crumpled like aluminium foil as it hit the cinder-smothered yard. In the midst of the ruin sat the hulk of a personnel carrier. Its armour was no longer the standard Soviet drab gray, now the exposed bare metal showed alternate bands of straw yellow and deep blue between smudges of black, like an inexpertly quenched machine-tool.

Kurt made no attempt to conceal his leering pleasure as he watched Andrea running toward them. Her camouflage jacket gave little evidence of the superb body beneath, but he could imagine it. The smooth round breasts would be bouncing at every step, fighting the restraints of her bra. She'd be sweating now, and he imagined what it would be like to rub his hard body down in the damp valley between them. Shit, he should have tied her down and fucked her when he had the chance. What tricks he could have taught her! But not now, not now they were with this crowd of Brits and Yanks—she had too many protectors.

Not that the bitch needed any, Ernst had found that out the hard way. Kurt still remembered the scream, and the sight of the would-be rapist as he staggered out of the house, his entrails hanging from his slashed stomach down into the trousers around his ankles. He'd have gone for her then, but none of the others would help. When Karl had almost met a similar fate a couple of nights later, and had been lucky only to lose the end of his penis, they had given up the idea of taking her by force and resigned themselves to a frustrating time, taking it out on the available women refugees when they could. Now he was the only one of the gang left.

They hated him, this lot. The major, the sergeant, all of them, just because he had been a border guard. He knew he was there on sufferance, and only because Andrea was. Still, it was better than a prison camp, that would have been the alternative, and they couldn't watch him forever. No point in escaping now, let them protect him, he'd make his break when they were out of the Zone, that was the best plan. But plan or no plan, if the war came to a sudden end then he would have to get out fast, lose himself among the millions of refugees. Remote though such a possibility seemed, it was one he had reason to fear. To the communists he was a deserter, to the West Germans a war criminal, his fate would be the same whichever side won and got him in their clutches.

If he ripped off all her clothes now she'd be good

and hot, nicely lubricated underneath, he'd be able to slip in easy, once her hands were tied. Just the thought made him leak . . .

Kurt took his eyes from the girl, as he realised the sniper's were on him. Nasty that one, cold, emotionless; even the big man, Dooley, was wary of him.

"Let's move." Revell added his urging to Hyde's. "We've got to find a clearing for the chopper to do a pick-up. Come on, shift."

"I'd rather walk." Cohen felt ill at the prospect of another ride. "Just give me a call and tell me where you're heading, I'll meet you there."

"If you can run at a couple of hundred kilometres an hour you're welcome." Hyde wiped rain from his face, and left a smear of mud across his disfigured features. "Otherwise shut up and get moving."

"You want me to take the radio?" Dooley extended a hand to the corporal.

"You can piss off. If I want help I'll want it reliable, and at reasonable rates. I'll stick to Avis."

"Suit yourself, just trying to be helpful." Giving Burke a nudge that pushed him an involuntary three steps sideways, Dooley lifted his own load.

"That major of yours is in a bloody hurry isn't he?" Burke rubbed his shoulder as they started off.

"He doesn't like the battle to go cold, likes to keep things on the boil." As they walked, Dooley interrupted the conversation to dart forward and lift a low branch to save Cohen from having to bend, showering him in water in the process.

"That'll be two marks," he called to the corporal as he fell back alongside Burke again. "Would have been five, but I'm giving a special introductory

78

offer." Dooley grinned at the inevitable obscenity he received in reply. "No extra charge for the shower." He took out a grimy scrap of paper, and with an equally filthy stub of a pencil noted the amount.

Burke took up again where he'd been forced to leave off. "That's alright while he's boiling Reds, like he's just done, but why's he in such a fucking hurry to see the same happen to us?"

"You're not dead yet, are you?"

"Not for want of bloody trying."

"Quit worrying, the Major will take care of us. I've been with him six months, and I ain't come to any harm."

"You mean you were a head-case when he first knew you?" Ducking just in time, Burke avoided the casually swung M16 that slashed through the leaves above him.

"I'm telling you," Dooley stabbed a finger the size of a salami toward Burke, "he's good, good at his job, good at looking after his men. The only difference between him and your sergeant is that he keeps pressing on, when that shitty gargoyle of yours would stand back and wait for the smoke to clear before having another go."

Burke dropped it. The big man had blind faith in his officer; it could be dangerous devotion in battle. There were lots of different reasons for obeying orders, but so far he'd found the most convincing one was that it avoided him having to do too much thinking himself. Sod it, there was no way he was ever going to get a stripe, so what was the point of putting on displays of initiative? In his lowly position it wasn't required of him, while officers and

79

NCOs were still on their feet, and by the time casualties forced him to take command of the section he'd be the only one left alive. Then there'd only be one order, and he could give that to himself while he was running.

"Want a hand?"

Recovering from the trip that had brought him to his knees, Burke treated Dooley's offer with suspicion. "I may be older than the rest of you, but not that much. Anyway I can't afford your rates."

"That's alright, no charge." Dooley took Burke's pack as he helped him up. "Just till you get your breath back."

Cohen had witnessed the incident. "So for him it's gratis?"

"It's for a buddy. You pass around a few of your diamonds and you'll have some. I'll be first in line."

There was no need for Cohen to pause to consider the suggestion. "In that case I'll die wealthy instead, lonely but wealthy." The radio crackled into life, and he hurried to catch up with the major as a message came in.

"What'll it be this time?" Dooley watched him threading his way forward.

"Whatever it is," Burke retrieved his pack, "I'll put money on your major turning it into a fight."

"No takers," Dooley hitched the M16 to a more comfortable position and patted his ammunition pouches. "No takers."

The Zone - Northern Sector

Attempts by the Royal Navy to sweep the Elbe estuary of mines, as a preliminary to forcing a passage to Hamburg, have been called off after the loss of the minesweepers HMS Brecon *and HMS* Middleton. *The modified torpedo recovery vessel RNAS* Tormentor *is on its way to the area, and it is thought attempts will be made by RN divers to recover one of the new Russian mines.*

Lieutenant General K. I. Pavloskii has been relieved of his command of the Soviet forces surrounding Hamburg, following the defeat of the third major assault in six weeks by the West German and British defenders. He is now in Moscow. His successor has not yet been announced. He will be the third to be appointed in five months. It is understood that there is no competition among the Russian General Staff for the post.

Polish and Hungarian divisions have now been

positively identified opposite the Hanover salient. The increased use of satellite forces on this most active front is thought to be due to two reasons:

ONE: The Russians' aim to reduce their own losses in experienced combat units, currently running at four per cent per week.

TWO: A desire to strengthen the "involvement" of other members of the Warsaw Pact by increasing their casualty lists.

The Cuban battalion operating with the Soviet 2nd Guards Army near Munster is now known to have suffered eighty-seven per cent casualties in two days of fighting with the 2nd Battalion of the RAF Regiment. British losses are put at one dead, two missing believed killed, seven wounded.

CHAPTER SIX

The little country town of Budlingen was close enough to the western fringes of the Zone to have suffered extensively from looting. Added to the dereliction brought about by almost two years of neglect and nature's unchecked advances, was the clutter of abandoned furniture and other goods outside virtually every shop and house. Most of it was weather-ravaged and scattered, but here and there stood neat stacks of televisions and other electrical applicances, still awaiting collection by gangs who had been unable or unwilling to return for them.

Tissue-thin wood veneer peeled from once polished cabinets, drooping down on to the clouded plastic covers of music centres. Grass and weeds flourished about and between them, adding an incongruous touch.

"These places give me the creeps." Dooley looked around warily as they stood waiting for Revell and the sergeant to return from scouting for suitable sites and premises. "It's no fucking wonder the refugees build their camps out in the country."

"Spooky or not, I'd rather have a decent roof over my head than live in one of the camps. A tent isn't any substitute for tiles." Rubbing accumulated grime from a shop window, Burke peered in at the dusty shelves. They were empty save for a few large wicker baskets that had held loaves long ago. A mouse scurried across a counter top, tumbling noiselessly to a bouncy landing on the floor, before hurrying from sight.

There was a loud bang. Everyone jumped as Dooley smashed his boot through the screen of a large colour set and was showered with thick fragments of glass. He ignored the shouts of protest. "I always wanted to do that."

"You're a bloody hooligan, a vandal." There was irritation in Libby's voice. "If you have to do bloody stupid things like that, do it thoroughly. Use your thick head next time."

"You want to start calling names, save it for the shits in the Kremlin who started the whole stinking business. They're the fucking vandals." Dooley had been about to hand out similar treatment to a second television, now he held back. "Fuck it, can't I even have a bit of fun without someone having a go at me. You lot get on my tits." He stalked away, kicking a Hoover from his path.

Clarence sat on a twin-tub washing machine, scraping every last speck of brick dust from his rifle, stripping the bullets from the magazines and cleaning each one individually. The tension that was getting to the others had not touched him. He finished the last checks, loaded the re-chambered Enfield and slowly took aim at a street sign two hundred metres away. An instant after firing, a large area of paint jumped from its face, as the heavy bullet punched through the center of the circle of sheet metal, deeply denting the post behind it. A second shot ploughed into a shop sign some yards further away and frosted glass and fluorescent tubes cascaded on to the path.

Satisfied, the sniper reloaded the magazine. The fight to come was more to his liking. Given good concealment, with just a little luck, he would push his score to over two hundred. It was a start. He had set the price of revenge at a hundred Russians for each member of his family. At his current rate he would achieve his target in about seven months. He had not as yet considered what he would do when he reached it. There would be time enough for that when it happened.

"Here we go again." Burke watched Revell and Hyde returning. "I'll be bleeding glad when we've used up the last of these things. Jesus but my arms ache." He prepared to pick up a case of reloads for their Dragon anti-tank rocket launchers. "I'm supposed to be a ruddy combat driver, not a sodding packmule."

"Be grateful we've got them. This scrap is going to be at close range, we'll be using the contraptions almost like bazookas, flight time will be too short for effective gathering and guidance. It'll be a case of see, point and fire."

"Is that supposed to cheer me up, Sarge?"

"No Burke, just keep you informed. You're always complaining no one ever tells you anything. Come to that you're always complaining."

For a moment Burke considered contesting the statement, but decided not to. "Well in future I'd rather stay ignorant, better for my peace of mind."

"OK Sergeant, let's get set up." Revell was counting the ammunition cases when he heard the approaching engines. A black staff car and a half-ton truck were coming down the main street. "Damn it, don't you know this road is closed? It's going to be full of T84s inside an hour." He shouted at the car's driver, who had pulled up nearby and had stuck his head out of the window.

"Good. I'm in the right place then." Not put off by the greeting, a young lieutenant climbed out, as an assortment of variously armed cooks, clerks and combat engineers jumped from the back of the truck.

"What the hell is this?" Revell looked on incredulously as the lieutenant had the new arrivals lifting cases of grenades and M72 Viper launchers from the truck.

Undeterred by the brusque demand, the lieutenant sauntered forward and threw a casual salute. "I heard there was a chance of a skirmish with stray Russian armour, so I rounded up some, eh, volunteers from the hangers-on around Corps HQ, borrowed the General's car and a truck the supply boys didn't seem to have too much use for, and motored out here looking for a slice of the action. When does the fun start. I'm not too late am I?"

*   *   *

86

"You sure you heard his name right. Lieutenant Hogg? He's not a grunt is he? You *sure* you heard the name right?"

"Sure I'm sure." Cohen was stung by Dooley's scepticism. "I heard him talking with the major. He's an engineer with 373rd Bridge Building Company. He was hanging about VII Corps HQ waiting for transport when he heard about us."

"I don't give a fuck what he's called. I just wish he'd stop smiling all the fucking time." By pretending to be making adjustments to the support legs of the Dragon missile launcher, Burke avoided helping the two Americans carry the sealed reload rounds in from the doorway. "It's fucking unnerving having someone around who grins like a bleeding Cheshire cat all the time. Where is he now?"

Broken glass from the smashed front of the hardware store crunched under heavy ammunition boxes as they were set down beside the launcher. Dooley took out one of the Dragon rounds and clipped it to the side of the sight-and-command module. "He's upstairs with the major."

"Shit, I didn't know that. Why didn't you bloody say something? I could have landed myself right in it."

"And miss the look on your face if he'd suddenly come back down and heard you!" The joke was being hugely enjoyed by Dooley. "I was hoping you might come out with an opinion or two on what you thought of officers, just to spice it up, make sure as much crap hit the fan as possible."

"You're bloody warped."

"Ain't we all." Dooley patted the launcher, set up

87

to fire out into the street. "Ain't we all?"

"We'll let about half the column pass by." In the thick dust of the table top Revell sketched the main street. "We've tried hitting the head twice, but with all that weight of armour and fire-power the Reds just charge straight through. I'm betting that if we chop off a large enough section of the tail, the vanguard will turn around and come back to help it out. If it works, we might be able to tie them up until late afternoon . . ."

Lieutenant Hogg bent over the crude map and doodled in details with the tip of his bayonet, occasionally glancing out of the window. "How many do you aim to knock out?"

"As many as we can, but I'm hoping we can hit the APCs first. Without infantry support the commie tanks are going to be at a disadvantage in these narrow streets. If they stay closed down they'll be as good as blind, if they open up we'll have snipers ready to knock off the commanders as they poke their heads out."

"You've what, thirty men? We'll parcel them out among our Dragon positions. That'll give my tank busters a chance to get on with their job without having to worry about any red infantry that survives to make trouble."

"Spread out on both sides of the street." Hogg examined the dotted-in anti-tank teams. "It's not going to be easy organising a withdrawal."

"There won't be any withdrawal. We'll slog it out until we've used all the Dragon rounds, then we'll mix it with M72s and finally finish them off with half bricks and two-by-fours if need be. You can change position if you have to, but maintain close contact at all times."

The words did nothing to wipe the smile of faint amusement from the lieutenant's face. If anything, it broadened a fraction more. "Do you mind if I ask what your exact orders are, Major? It seems to me, from the impression I got before I came out here, that you were just to harass and delay the column, not try to finish it off single-handedly."

"Your impression's near enough correct, but I've got my own way of 'harassing' enemy armour. You didn't have to come, and you don't have to stay."

"Oh I'm staying, Major." Hogg patted the grenades clipped to his belt. "I'm not sporting these babies because I think they look pretty. I've got fed up with shoving bridge sections around while commie artillery shovel stinking mud all over me. Now I reckon I'm about due to get a bit of my own back. Here will do as well as anywhere."

"OK, so long as you're happy, and you look like you are," Hogg's permanent grin was beginning to grate on Revell, "let's get on with it. First we'll sort your men out. It'll spoil the surprise if they're still milling about like a load of lost sheep when the lead T84 arrives, and that could be soon." A thought struck the major, though he half-suspected it had been hovering at the back of his mind and he'd unconsciously suppressed it until now, when it could be put off no longer. "You fought tanks before?"

Now why the hell had the major had to ask that?

89

Hogg saw the interrogative look aimed at him. Oh what the hell . . . "Not exactly . . . I guess . . . no." Brother, did that sound lame, even to him. Heck, so what, this hard bastard wasn't going to turn him away, he needed the help. "We've all got to learn sometime, Major. Shall I set up my men now?"

"Yes, get on it. Make sure there's a good mix of weapons at each strongpoint. I'll be along in a minute." Cannon fodder. It was a term Revell had always despised, and one he'd always sworn would never be applied to any men under his command. Now, as he heard Hogg descending the stairs, he crossed to the window and looked out at the newcomers.

They were typical of the hangers-on, super-numeraries and supplicants to be found skulking about any large headquarters. A good third were obviously veterans, men who'd been trying to locate their units, and having lost patience with a staff too busy with other matters to help, had opted to join the lieutenant's expedition as an alternative to kicking their heels.

Another ten or so were painfully conspicuous. Uniforms as yet unsoiled, clutching factory-fresh M16s, they somehow had an air of ignorance and eagerness. They might have stepped off the plane only an hour or two before. If that was the case, then from now on jet lag was going to be the least of their problems. Within an hour at the most, they were going to get a crash course in total warfare.

It was among the last ten that Revell noticed one or two soldiers who did not appear entirely happy with their situation or surroundings. It crossed his mind to wonder just how many of that contingent had actually gone through the formal process of volunteering. Included in their number were a few who bore the stamp of men well versed in the arts and skills of keeping out of officers' paths—and the firing line. Flushing them from hiding, from their card games, their bolt holes, would not have been easy. Their presence on the battlefield indicated the existence of qualities in Hogg that Revell would not have expected, judging from their short acquaintance.

If a man was going to turn and run though when the fight got nasty, it wasn't certain he'd be from that last group. Sometimes it was the veteran of twenty or more actions who broke under the strain. The shysters would measure the risks and, unless a building was burning around them, would stay put and keep their heads down. The youngsters would muddle through, probably supported and encouraged by more experienced men, like Cohen, who always saw himself as a father figure, although he was only in his mid-twenties. And if one of those kids did fail the test, then most likely he'd freeze, or do something real stupid and, either way, die so fast no one would ever know.

Every man had his breaking point, those who lived to reach it swelled the numbers suffering from battle exhaustion to over twenty per cent of all casualties. This war, more than any other, had proved itself capable of wounding minds as freely and as savagely as it did bodies.

Revell knew that if no bomb or bullet found him first, sooner or later he'd be joining the neurotics in the army's many psychiatric hospitals. It might happen suddenly, without any warning, or if he was alert he'd detect the minor symptoms developing: the nightmares and consequent fear of sleep, or maybe hypersensitivity to shellfire, or exaggerated caution in action. If he turned himself over to the shrinks in time, he'd be among the third who made it back into the line, if he was lucky—if that was being lucky.

He could see that Hogg had just about sorted his men out, and picking up his 12-gauge assault shotgun he went to check the arrangements. It felt comfortable in his grasp as he started down to the street. He'd long since grown accustomed to its weight, accepting that penalty in exchange for its murderous effectiveness in close combat situations, where the edge it gave him had saved his life on several occasions.

"Cohen, with me. Find out how much longer we've that prowler overhead. It must be near the limit of its endurance." Without waiting for the radio-man, Revell strode out into the street. The rain had stopped, and fitful bursts of sunlight slanting through gaps in the overcast sky made the buildings and road surface sparkle.

"What do you want to do with this?" Hogg indicated the multi-barrelled mini-gun in the back of the truck.

"How many rounds did you bring? One burp of fire and that could chuck all the lead we've got."

"About six thousand, mostly armour-piercing incendiary, enough for a couple of minutes if we take it easy." Jumping into the back of the vehicle, Hogg pulled aside a sheet, revealing a pile of large ammunition cases and the small generator which provided power for the gun's motor.

"Good, that we can use." Revell looked down the street to where, several blocks away, the other two Dragon teams were set up and waiting. In his mind's eye he pictured their field of fire, and then that of the weapon in the hardware store at the top of the street. "We'll set it up here, but it's too late to emplace it. Clamp it to the bed of the truck, then drive the whole rig into one of these side streets so it can fire out. I've got a man who's expert with these. I'll send him along. He'll need two loaders, and there'd better be a driver in the cab for a quick shift of position if it's needed."

"And where do you want me?" It was a question whose answer Hogg couldn't anticipate, but he wasn't about to let the uncertainty hovering over his part in the ambush dampen his feelings. Hell, he felt good just being here, just being involved. Let the other guys build bridges, he was going to do some real fighting.

"You're in charge up this end. The Russians will pass you first. Keep your men out of sight, don't open up until I do, then hit the rear of the column as hard as you can. If it all goes right, then between our two positions we should bottle-up about a third of the column. I can stop them going on, you can prevent them turning around and Hyde's Dragon and the mini-gun can hammer what's trapped between us."

"Sounds fun. We should be able to take care of them."

93

"You'll have to. I'll have my hands full taking care of the lead armour when it turns around and comes charging back to bail out what we've got trapped." By now Revell didn't expect anything to wipe the idiot smirk off the lieutenant's face. "Any word from the ECM platform yet?"

"Got it now, Major. Just signing off." Cohen sat on a huge hi-fi speaker, the radio resting on its twin. "He's got a full set of ferry tanks, so we've got him for another ninety minutes yet."

"That should be long enough."

"Hope you're right, Major. The guys up there say they've been playing ring-a-roses with relays of Hind helicopter gunships for the last half hour. When he goes, they come. Can we be a few miles from here when they do?"

"What makes you think we'll be in any condition to travel by then?"

Cohen made to answer the lieutenant, but decided against it even as he opened his mouth. His stripes were new, they'd leave no telltale mark if they were removed, but he didn't see any reason to invite their loss so soon. So the extra pay didn't amount to much saved for a year, it wouldn't equal what he could make in an hour in one of the refugee camps. But money was money, and he wasn't about to throw it away. And besides, he liked being a corporal; maybe he didn't rate a staff car and yards of gold braid, but it was a start. He tagged along as Revell led his contingent of the lieutenant's men toward the south end of the main street.

Sergeant Hyde was putting the finishing touches to a carelessly piled barricade of shopfittings, concealing a missile launcher inside a gutted delicatessen. Next door, the semi-naked dummies in a dress shop window added a touch of absurdity to the war-like preparations.

"I'll be taking over Libby's Dragon at the south end of the street. There's a mini-gun up the road needs his touch." Without waiting for any comment from the British NCO, Revell set about dispersing the newcomers to the pre-selected positions.

Waiting until the last of his men had left to assume their fire posts, Hyde marched up to the officer. Before speaking he made it clear with a jerk of his thumb that he didn't want Cohen nearby.

"Are you sure that's a good idea, Major? You can't take out tanks and direct the action at the same time."

"Once the shooting starts, Sergeant, there won't be any need for orders. The men have their places, all they have to do is hold them. This is our last chance to hit the column inside the Zone: if everyone does just that, hits it and hits it hard, then there's nothing else to be added. And besides, I'll be more useful on that launcher than I will be sitting on my butt trying to make out what's going on through a pea-soup obscuration of smoke and dust, shouting orders that aren't needed to soldiers who haven't time to listen. You ever done street fighting?"

The question instantly put Hyde on his guard. "Yes, some, six weeks in Grosshansdorf, outside Hamburg."

"I heard that was a real rough house . . . so you'll know what it's all about. Was that before the Russians closed in, or had the siege already started then?"

"We were rotated a couple of days before the Elbe was mined, got out just in time."

Hyde knew what it was all about. Street fighting ... grenades and flame-throwers, bayonets and booby traps. Fast, fluid and dirty, that just about summed it up, especially dirty ...

CHAPTER SEVEN

Clarence put his hand out and pushed. The big gilded eagle rocked. He pushed again, harder, and this time the heavy cast lectern toppled and hit the floor beside the altar with a loud crash that echoed and rumbled through the church, bringing curtain-like falls of dust from the arched ceiling high overhead.

"Does that make you feel better?" Andrea stood in a small doorway set into a corner of the wall, partially concealed by a faded red velvet drape. "This leads to the tower. There is a good view, much of the main street, the side roads as well. Are you coming, or do you wish to break the windows also? Perhaps tear the Bible with your teeth, if it helps."

There was no detectable mockery in her tone. Fitting one of the dum-dum clips into his rifle, the sniper put three fast shots into the richly illuminated brass-bound book making a tent on the floor. Despite its weight it spun away under the impact, the second and third bullets sending up a shower of torn pages and shreds of tooled black leather. "These are my teeth." He removed the magazine, replaced the spent rounds with loose ones from his pocket and snapped it back in.

"They bite well. Shall we eat some Russians?" She led the way up the narrow staircase.

The walls were cold and damp to the touch; cobwebs held away from the stones by the draught reached for them, clinging to their clothes and weapons. Andrea shied from those flapping at her face, turning them aside with the barrel of her M16. The angular automatic rifle looked huge in her small hands, against her slight frame, but she carried it effortlessly, in addition to fifteen grenades for its underslung launcher and the big 9mm Walther P5 pistol worn low on her right hip.

"This'll do." Clarence called a halt on reaching the platform below the bell chamber, and examined the town through the louvred windows.

"We can go higher. It will give us a better field of fire."

"So it will, and make us better targets." He moved over to the next flight of stairs and blocked her way as she made to go on up. "As soon as those commies come under sniper fire, the first thing they're going to do is look for our likely hiding place. It won't take them long to include the tower among the list of likely candidates. And being Russians they'll blast the top of it, just in case. That'll be fine by us, because all we'll be doing is sitting tight a couple of flights down, waiting for them to finish wasting ammo. Soon as the excitement is over, we pop up again and go on making life dangerous for them."

"I did not think you were concerned about living."

"I'm not, but I am bothered about dying. I've too much to do, I don't want to go just yet. Your trouble is the same as the major's, you're too keen, you take unnecessary risks. He fancies you, did you know that?"

"Of course." Taking off her helmet, Andrea let her dark chestnut hair fall to her shoulders, making no attempt to straighten it. "Does it bother you? It should not. I know men find me attractive, I do not seek to have that effect, but sometimes it can be useful. Would the major have fought to keep me in his unit if I had been ugly? Of course he would not."

"If ever any of them bother you too much, go too far, I'll take care of them. I know there are always some who try it on, but . . ."

"Of myself I can take care, but why do you offer?" Using the butt of her rifle, she smashed one of the wooden slats to make a wider firing aperture. "You are not interested in me. You have never tried to touch me."

"I . . . I don't really know. Perhaps I just want someone to care about again. That must sound rather weak, and silly."

"No, I can understand. You have lost much, and though you would like to, you have not been able to cut yourself off from your emotions completely. Everyone has a need, even the Russians, though with them it is a need to oppress, enslave."

"What's your need? Some of the men think you are a lesbian. As I won't talk about our relationship they're making up their own stories."

"If you told them how it was between us, they

99

would not believe you. For them a man and a woman together means only one thing. I am not concerned by what they think. Let them weave their fantasies, they do me no harm." Over the iron sights of the M16 Andrea took in every detail of the town spread out below, searching for the likely places where baled-out tank crews might first seek shelter.

"You avoided the question. Come on, you've analysed me, tell me what your need is; why the hell are you in this war?" Clarence took out a small square of cleaning cloth and began to polish the lens of his telescopic sight.

"Why? Because the communists started a war and I could not help being involved in it. If I had not joined the Workers Militia I might have been forced into a labour battalion, perhaps sent to the armament factories beneath the forests of Siberia. Many East Germans were."

"But why stay in?" Clarence pressed the point. "When you deserted you could have mingled with the refugees, tried to work your way west. Why join Kurt and that band of cut-throat border guards?"

"I joined the Grepos because they were better armed than the other gangs infesting the camps, because with them I could be sure of getting food, of living. How many refugees ever make it across the Zone? I tell you, one tenth of one per cent, and as a woman alone my chances would have been lower than that."

She had avoided the question again. He wouldn't try a third time. Perhaps she would tell him eventually. Although they'd been working as a team for a month now, it was the first time they had exchanged any words other than those essential to whatever they were doing. She was right about Dooley and the others not understanding how it was between them.

The fact that Andrea was attractive in all the right places would have made it even less possible for them to comprehend the non-physical nature of their relationship. Perhaps if they knew about his impotence . . . but that wasn't something he was going to shout about. That concerned no one but him.

They'd told him at the hospital he'd get over it. So soon after his wife's death it hadn't been important, had even been a help. Now he'd adjusted to it, accepted it. There might be a time in the future when it would worry him, but he couldn't really believe he had a future. How many of the combatants in the Zone had?

"Everything is ready." Andrea watched the last of the preparations in the main street. "We must hope that the major is correct."

"I should think that he is. The Russians have to come this way, unless they take to the side roads, and that's not too likely. They'll have lost enough time already, they daren't risk getting lost."

"It is strange that men who are going to die should be in a hurry."

"Not really. Everything the commies have ever done is based on bullying. When you do that hard enough the result is terror, and that is apt to make you blind before it kills you."

"Let me do it." After watching for a couple of

minutes Libby grew exasperated with the youngster's ineffective attempts to secure the tripod clamp, and did it himself. He tested the mini-gun mount for stability, then switched on the power. The cluster of barrels spun smoothly, almost silently. An adjustment to the rate of fire control and they blurred into rushing gray invisibility.

"Too fast." Altering the fire selector to one thousand rounds a minute, Libby also pre-set the burst control at one hundred. "No point in using up all the goodies at once. Might as well be generous and spread these about a bit." He lifted the end of the snaking belt of linked rounds and fed it into the side of the weapon. "All you two have to do," he stabbed a finger at the young clerks who'd been appointed his loaders, "is to bring up fresh boxes as I call for them, get the empties out of my way as fast as you can and relay any instruction to that heavy-footed clown in the cab. You," he pointed to the younger of the pair, "what's your name?"

"Ripper, eh . . . This here is Wilson, we're both from . . ."

"I don't want your life history. Just one of you tell leadfoot to stop gunning that bloody engine. I don't want it to damned well seize just when we need it."

While Wilson went off to pass on the message through the hatch in the cab roof, Ripper examined the gun, being careful not to touch it, wary of Libby's critical glare. "Sure is a fancy iron. Beats the old fowling piece I had back home. I come from . . ."

"Bring up another box and have it ready will you." The southern drawl grated on Libby. Until the war had come along, the only contact he'd had with

Americans, if it could be called that, was via the TV. Of the mass of imported programmes, just two had made him grind his teeth and reach for the channel tuner. Until now he'd never really believed there actually were people who talked like the characters in *Barnaby Jones* or *Dallas*. And now he had two live specimens working with him. At least, he thought he had two. He couldn't be sure about Wilson. The gangling carrot-top with galloping acne was just a shade less chatty than Kurt, and *he* averaged only three grunts a day, on good days.

"I've not seen one of these before, how do they handle? I mean, are they difficult, what with vibration an' all?"

"Not if they're carefully mounted. This is a bit makeshift, but at this rate of fire it'll do." If Ripper was angling to sit behind the Gatling-type gun, Libby was going to disappoint him. The last thing he wanted was a hick clown tampering with things he didn't understand. Ripper still hovered, he was chewing his lip and contriving to somehow give the impression that he was hopping up and down while he hunched over the gun's barrels. He kept giving Libby weird smiles, in which only the bottom half of his face participated, mainly by exposing masses of tiny teeth. There appeared to be enough for several normal mouths. The youngster was painfully thin, and his helmet, perched above sharp bird-like features, looked about three sizes too large, slumping first over one ear, then the other, then down over his eyes.

"Could you knock out a tank with one of these, for real?"

"Only if I was firing it inside." Oh bugger it, it was a serious question, not too intelligent, but serious. "No, I'll be going for the personnel carriers. Concentrating bursts on one section of their armour, I should be able to put a few rounds into them, and that's all it takes."

"You mean these little bitty bullets can stop an APC?" Ripper prodded the rounds in the belt like a Pacific Islander being offered his first trade beads.

"More likely they'll buzz about inside chopping the crew to pieces, but they've got an incendiary filling, so they could ignite fuel, or set off ammo racks."

"Well I'll be, ain't that something . . ."

Wilson had at last managed to catch the attention of their driver by taking his rifle and pounding it up and down on the man's helmet. For whatever reason, the engine revs suddenly fell away and the whole truck stopped rattling in time to the straining power unit.

"This is the first time I've been in action, same goes for Wilson here, don't it, Wilson?" Ripper didn't wait for confirmation. "See we figured, as the war's gonna end soon anyway . . ."

"Now where the hell did you get that?" Libby was silenced by a knowing wink from Ripper.

"Ah know." He sank his voice to a conspiratorial whisper. "Ah know because my cousin John, he sells fresh dog meat."

The relevance of that particular authority was lost on Libby. He tried to think of a polite way to voice the query. "What the fuck has that got to do with the end of the war?" and failed.

Again the long slow wink. "One of his very best customers is Old George." If he expected light to suddenly dawn on Libby's face he suffered a letdown. Ripper elaborated. "Old George, Old George who used to be a gardener at the State Governor's mansion. Like he says, he may not be right at the hub of things no more, but he still gets all the low-down, keeps his fingers on the pulse of the nation as he says. That's how my cousin John . . ."

"Who sells the fresh dog meat . . ."

"Right, you're with me now. That's how he heard from Old George that the Governor had said to one of the maids how the war was gonna end any time. And as he was only half-drunk and getting real horny with her at the time, it must be the truth."

"Fascinating. I suppose we might as well pack up and go home now." It took an effort for Libby not to laugh out loud, especially as Ripper's face was a picture of earnestness, and was mirrored by the silent Wilson's.

"You'll have to put off your departure, at least for an hour." Lieutenant Hogg stuck his beaming face round the side of the truck. "Seems like there's a Russian column coming who don't have access to such interesting inside information, and we might just have to restrain them. That OK with you, Ripper?"

"Fine by me, Lieutenant. Like I was telling this fella here, before I got sidetracked, me and Wilson we wanted to get in on the action and get ourselves a medal or two before it was all over. We'd have felt a mite foolish if we'd stepped off the plane, been told it'd ended and that we were going back on the next flight."

"I see your point." Hogg turned to Libby. "Don't open up until you hear the Dragons go into action. And if you're forced to shift position, don't park anywhere near the big building two blocks down. The combat engineers brought a few kilos of explosive with them and we've mined the place. Good luck."

"Hey, now don't he seem a nice fella." Ripper watched the lieutenant depart. "Boot camp would have been a touch more pleasant if a handful of our drill sergeants had been like him."

Wilson didn't say anything, but his slow nod signalled agreement.

Libby rubbed his brow, he had one hell of a headache coming on. He could only pray that the Russians would oblige him by removing its cause. The two southerners were sharing a bar of chocolate, blissfully unaware of the prayer being aimed at them. Wincing at a sharp and painful twinge in his left temple, Libby added a rider to the supplication; he uttered it out loud, though under his breath, to give it added force and weight. "And please, make it soon."

"He's chasing about like a blue-arsed fly out there." Burke watched the lieutenant dashing from one building to another, checking his men were in place. "He sure is a worker, just the sort we don't want in this outfit."

106

"Fuck him, what we need is a chef." Loud rumblings were coming from Dooley's large gut. "At the moment I'd even settle for the crummiest short order cook in the States, even an army cook, third class."

"Christ, you must be bloody hungry to wish that on yourself. I'd hesitate before wishing that on a shitty commissar." Nibbling at the corner of a block of K-rations, Burke attempted to figure out precisely what it was, or was supposed to be. He didn't succeed.

"What makes it all the fucking worse," Dooley paused to listen to a particularly angry burst of sound from beneath his belt. "Will you listen to that, it's fucking tearing itself apart. . . . What's making it all the worse, is that a couple of hours drive from here is some of the most incredible fucking food you ever tasted. You like German dishes?"

"Only the ones with skirts on."

"No, you shit; the food." Checking his food pack for the tenth time, and shaking out and licking the last imagined crumb from his grubby palm, Dooley hurled it away in disgust. "What I need is one of the sausages like they do at the Alt Nurnberg, washed down with a gallon of beer, or a Zepplinwurst, or," he licked his lips and slurped appreciatively, "pickled pork ribs or breaded pork chops . . ."

"You've eaten so many pigs you're starting to turn into one."

"Shut up, Burke, you old misery. I tell you, I can see why the West German army is so fucking fanatical. Any country that can produce beer, wine and food like this does has got to be worth fighting

107

for. When this lot is over I'm staying. I'll get a little farm, somewhere round here maybe, and keep pigs. I'll grow pork, old and fat."

"And shack up with some fat-arsed old frau."

"And why not? I like my women big, like to feel a good pair of haunches grinding into my lap when I take them from behind, and plenty of udder up front to give good hand holds."

"Big is one thing. I saw that piece you picked up on Munchener Strasse. She was twice your age, sixty if she was a day. I wouldn't have known which bloody wrinkle to part to shove it in; from the front *or* back."

Dooley made pitying noises. "I had a fucking good session with that one. This is where you go wrong, you pick up the youngest bit you can. Apart from the fact it's like trying to shove your tool into a mouse's earhole, they're always so unimaginative, and they're usually surly or downright disinterested. Oh I've had young'uns, but for all the bloody fun it was I might just as well have stuffed it into the neck of a Coke bottle."

Crossing to the door, Burke looked out, in the direction from which the Russian column would be coming. "Should be any time now. I'm bloody glad this is the last ambush. HQ must have scraped together a blocking force by now, they must have, even if they had to swipe tanks from the delivery squadrons." He came back into the room. "Alright, so tell me what's so good about wrinkled old hags. I'm listening."

"Next time you start looking for a pick-up, just

start looking properly. For a start, the older ones have usually taken a bit of care over their appearance, got done up. That makes a change from fucking jeans and T-shirts. OK, so young nipples look good, but there's a lot to be said for a well-filled corset as well. Another thing, if they're past their best they're always grateful, and they show it in a lot of ways. I've had good screws and good presents; this watch for one." Rolling back his cuff, Dooley showed the big black and white dial of the Brietling Chronograph. "What have you ever had from the young'uns except verbal buckets of cold water if they suddenly don't feel like it, or a dose of the clap?"

"Maybe you've got a point, but . . ."

"There's no fucking buts about it, I'm right. I tell you what, next forty-eight hour leave we get I'll introduce you to Anna. Beautiful broad, about fifty; tits you wouldn't believe, right out here. If you don't watch out she'll suck you in and blow you out in bubbles. It'll be an experience you'll never forget."

"I don't doubt that." He wasn't quite certain how he'd got into this, but one thing was for sure, Burke was going to get out of it. Fifty! Ugh, it was bad enough growing old himself, without burying himself to his balls in something even older. Christ, he just had to get out of it somehow. Still, it was a worry he could shunt to one side for the moment; after the coming battle there might be nothing left for him to worry about; there might be nothing left of him.

*   *   *

Hyde could hear the machine gun crew moving about directly overhead. He hadn't had much chance to talk to them, but he could tell they knew what it was all about. Tank busting was dodgy at such short ranges, a well manned support weapon for close-in defence was very welcome. There were two more across the way, and another lower down, flanking the major's Dragon position.

The time dragged slowly; it would have helped if he'd had someone to talk to, but there was only Kurt. The Grepo was picking his nose, rolling the pieces between his filthy fingers, then inspecting them before flicking them out into the street.

They were two ugly people together, Hyde knew that. Kurt because of who he was and what he'd been, and himself because of the way he was now. He put his hand to his face. His face! That was a joke. It wasn't his face, it was a hundred different parts of him, made up of the masses of tiny patches taken from all over his body during the twenty-five grafting operations. What a couple ... a monster and a horror.

"Why do you look at me?" Kurt stopped his nasal excavations.

Hyde ignored him, not bothering to answer. It would probably have been futile anyway, the East German's smattering of English wasn't up to coping with anything more complex than simple commands. Not that he would have talked to him even if it had been otherwise; none of them had time for the Grepo. Beyond the unpleasantness of the individual himself lay the evil reputation of the outfit from which he originated.

The sergeant knew that Kurt had only been kept with the unit to justify retaining the girl. It was a price Hyde wouldn't have paid for her continued company, attractive though she was.

"I think we got business." Kurt strained forward to look out, and listened intently. He knelt and put his ear to the ground. "Ya, we got business. Now we open a meat shop, ya?" His laugh was an ugly sound, as he drew his finger slowly across his throat.

CHAPTER EIGHT

The Soviet column was still travelling fast, making no concession to changes in the terrain or its surroundings. One after another, Revell watched the huge tanks and self-propelled guns thunder into his sights, saw the cross-hairs centre first on their broad frontal armour, then on their threshing tracks and mud-spattered road wheels. He was counting, ticking off each one in his mind and waiting for the first of the personnel carriers.

Every component of the building's fabric shook as the steel Leviathans pounded past. The last few shards of glass tinkled from the trembling frames and plaster fell from the walls and ceilings.

Twenty. Damn it, it had to be soon. Twenty-one, any moment now . . . the range was insanely short . . . it was a hell of a gamble . . . would the missile's thirty-two miniature thruster rockets lift it high enough after it popped from the tube . . . would it climb close enough to the line of sight on which he was aiming to score a vital hit?

Twenty-two. A long gap that time, sloppy station keeping. Twenty-three, another confounded self-propelled gun. Twenty-four . . . this was it. His thumb crushed down hard on the firing button and he felt the heat of the back blast.

Filling the shop with dust, the roaring tongue of recoil-cancelling gas and flame sent a great cloud of it billowing out into the street. The Dragon's position was instantly betrayed, but for the APC it was already too late.

Twin threads of wire unreeling behind it, the anti-tank round skimmed the road toward its target, climbing and accelerating as it went. Revell had the command unit aligned on the vehicle's front, just below the sharp angle made by its hull top and glacis plate: actual impact was a metre to one side of that, on its left track.

White smoke, giant orange sparks and flying fragments filled the street, and throwing its severed track out behind it the disabled vehicle slewed across the road and smashed into the front of a bank. Huge chunks of masonry fell on to the hull.

"Go get 'em, Major." Cohen snapped a reload into place as a second carrier raced out of the smoke, pumping high explosive shells indiscriminately from its turret gun and spitting tracer from every weapon port.

There was hardly time for Revell to aim. At even closer range than the first shot, there was little chance of the powerful warhead impacting against the APC's hull, and it didn't. He watched it spurt into the dark gap between the road and the vehicle's bellyplate. The result was as spectacular as it was unexpected.

With a shattering report the APC was lifted high off the ground, to fall back and lurch a couple of metres on distorted track and buckled wheels, then stall and present a perfect sitting target. It was an opportunity the major wouldn't pass up.

As hatches flew open and the escaping crew and infantry were met by a hail of machine gun fire, Revell took his time and, with the front feet of the Dragon tripod packed to give extra elevation, fired a third round.

The massive shaped charge effortlessly defeated the thin spaced armour of the APC's hull side and sent a jet of molten metal into its interior as the last of the Russians attempted to escape. Bodies, fuel and ammunition blazed.

From behind the flaming roadblock came further sounds of battle, as the other Dragon teams went to work on the concertinaed rear of the column. Clearly distinguishable above every other noise was the ripping-calico snarl of the mini-gun.

Cohen listened, as he offered the officer a further reload. "I'm glad I'm on this side of the roadblock. What they have back there is a problem."

"It's nothing to the one we'll have if the whole of the head of the column does an about turn and comes back. I counted more than twenty pieces of heavy armour. How many anti-tank rounds have we left?"

There was a pause while Cohen set aside two fragmentaiton rounds and a pair with high explosive warheads. "I make it ten, you want me to check again?"

"No." Revell looked out at the bodies strewn about

the burning APC, and at the thick black cloud swirling from it, carrying the repugnant stench of scorching flesh. "No, you couldn't make it thirteen more, and you might make it one less. Let's settle for what we've got."

Beyond the knocked-out vehicles the fight was becoming fiercer, indicated by the growing crash and clatter of cannon and automatic fire. A single high-pitched wailing scream was briefly audible, only to be drowned by a closely spaced series of explosions, as a heavy tank gun opened up rapid fire on the buildings flanking the street.

"Yeah," Cohen picked up his M16, "yeah, I'll settle for what we've got."

Libby hit the over-ride and sent a two hundred round burst at the APC, as it stopped across the entrance to the side road and its squat turret began to traverse toward them. He clearly saw the bullets' massed impacts on the hull side and track-guard, marked by puffs of white smoke and shortlived spurts of flame.

"Ya-hoo, you done got the bastard." Ripper leapt up and down waving his helmet above his head, then dived for cover and jammed it back on as the vehicle's gunner snapped off a hurried shot that passed uncomfortably close. "Hey, shit. He ain't supposed to do that, we got him first." There was intense indignation in his voice. "You hit him again now, that fella's cheating I tell you."

"There's no rule book in the Zone. Tell lead-foot to get ready for a fast exit." Using the last of the belt, Libby sent a second fusillade against the personnel

116

carrier's turret front, and its short-barrelled main gun immediately jerked to maximum elevation and stayed there.

"Hey, will you look at them go." Ripper stood and watched the Russian crew and infantry bale out, as smoke began to wreathe their transport, then had to jump to one side to avoid a savage kick from Libby.

"Don't just bloody look at them, kill them."

"Shit, there's no need to get nasty, I was going to." Belatedly, almost casually, Ripper shouldered his M16 and snapped off fast single shots at the escaping enemy.

Only two men made it to cover. With just eight shots they'd hardly seemed to aim, Wilson and Ripper had brought down eight Russians.

A long slow whistle escaped Libby. "We've got a sniper you should meet."

"Heck, we'd be no good at that." As usual Ripper spoke for the two of them. "We just like to pick up a gun and fire. I guess that's why our instructor on the range didn't take too kindly to us. All that lying down and doing it by numbers, for us it just kinda took all the fun out of it."

From the direction of the main street came the bellow of engines and the crash and rattle of various calibre weapons. Occasionally a spent bullet would ricochet into the side street, one of them clanging to a stop against an empty ammunition box on the truck.

"This party sure seems to be warming up a piece. Hows about we find ourselves a spot where we can join in the fun?"

"We're just about to." Moving to the back of the cab, Libby shouted in to the driver. "Find us another alley, close as you can." He had to grab hold of the roof hatch as the big six-wheeler surged forward under astounding acceleration for its size. The gearbox paid the price for the abuse, howling a protest as it was further punished by a clumsy shift.

As they pulled away, a 125mm tank shell burst through the front of a house and detonated against another across the street, punching a huge hole and dumping a torrent of brickwork across the spot they'd recently occupied.

Half a block further down, a narrow service entrance offered an opening just wide enough to accept the truck. Libby had their enthusiastic if none too skilful driver reverse them in, until the only thing between them and the main street was a tall spike-topped, double gate.

In the middle of the road sat a pair of T84s. One of them would never move again; a neat circular hole in its turret side was edged with beads of bright metal and the body of its driver sprawled from a hatch, draped over the sloped armour, his fingers brushing the ground. The other tank was closed down tight, its long cannon systematically pumping shells at a steady rate into the façade of the nearest buildings.

Further along, a multiple-barrelled Shilka flak-tank was handing out similar treatment to the structures nearest it. The much lighter 23mm rounds didn't pack the same punch as the T84's 125mm shells, but what they lacked in weight they made up for in quantity. Building after building was sprayed with a storm of high velocity projectiles that tore its frontage apart.

Knots of Russian infantry followed the barrage

ready to receive any prey flushed out. They moved cautiously, running bent double from doorway to doorway. As Libby watched, a slab-faced junior sergeant leading a small group reared up clutching at his chest, then toppled backwards on to the men crowding the doorway behind him. Another of the group fell, and as a survivor pointed up toward a church tower a rifle grenade landed among them.

Limbs and ragged scraps of equipment flew across the road. An officer attempting to rally another squad was hit and fell to his knees, before pitching forward on to his face. His men broke and ran, two more going down before they could find better shelter.

A Dragon missile arced from a shop front and, missing the still active tank, executed a tight turn toward the Shilka, but the manoeuvre demanded too much of the control surfaces. A flick-out fin broke off under the stress and it flopped to the ground to plough a furrow-like crater in the road surface.

"If we stick our noses out there we're going to get them shot off." There was no way that Libby could see of bringing the mini-gun into play without instantly attracting a great weight of enemy fire, and in the unarmoured truck that could have only one consequence. The brick walls to either side would offer no impediment to the steel-defeating rounds of the Soviet guns.

"Then let's get somewhere where we can. I didn't come out here for the purpose of sightseeing. I was hoping to participate." Ripper peered over the top of the gate, then ducked back swiftly as a bullet tore out one of the spikes beside him. "But I get your drift about this maybe not being the best location we could've picked."

More Russian armour was moving into view. A pair of self-propelled guns closely following a modified T72. Its main gun had been replaced with a large calibre mortar for demolition work, and it sported a full width bulldozer blade. A Dragon detonated harmlessly against the great steel crescent, and the self-propelled guns fanned out to hug the opposite side of the street.

Ripper and Libby exchanged looks, then Libby dropped down to man the mini-gun while the American clung to the gate, watching the approaching vehicles.

Selecting the highest rate of fire, Libby waited for the word. Above the roar of the battle he made out the growl of the approaching SP gun. It grew louder and its tracks could be heard squealing on the hard surface as its driver made fractional changes of course.

"He's all yours." Ripper jumped down as the engine note reached a crescendo.

Four hundred armour-piercing incendiary rounds went through the thick timber of the gate as if it wasn't there, striking the front of the vehicle as it drew level. It stopped instantly, and the driver's escape hatch was thrown open as blue smoke curled from the access panels of the engine positioned beside him.

"Move it." There was time to lob a couple of blast grenades blindly over the gate, and then Libby was once more hanging on for dear life as their maniac driver bounced the truck from one wall to another, racing down the service road and into the back street.

"Kinda exciting ain't it?" Hot shit, Ripper hadn't had so much fun in years, well not since he'd been drafted. The folks back home had it all wrong about this war, the Zone was a hell of a place. If he'd have know it was like this, he might not've waited for the letter from Uncle Sam.

The truck skidded round a corner, the driver fighting to get into gear, any gear, and piled head-on into a Russian APC. The shock of the collision threw everyone onto the floor. It was the turret gunner aboard the carrier who was fastest off the mark. At point-blank range he hosed the truck with heavy machine gun fire.

"I hope Hyde and the major are having fun down by the roadblock, it's fucking murder here." Clasping his hands tight over his head, Dooley stayed down on the floor as a third tank shell passed through the building, to detonate somewhere in its rear.

"Whose bloody murder, that's the thing?" At his second attempt, Burke managed to haul the Dragon from beneath the pile of debris and examined it. Little more than a glance told him it was beyond repair. "What do you say we get out of here?"

"I say yeah." Dooley risked raising his head. The T84 was still stationed right outside, but at last seemed to be turning its attention to other targets. "And let's make it now."

In several places the weight of the collapsed upper floors had brought the ceiling down, and they constantly had to climb over heaps of rubble, between precariously balanced and tottering partition walls. The bodies of two of Hogg's men, mutilated beyond recognition, had come down with the upper floors and formed a further gruesome obstruction to be clambered over. A stockless machine gun and crushed ammunition belts lay nearby.

"Hold it." Burke paused before venturing out. "Could be a reception committee waiting for us."

Without hesitating, Dooley took a grenade and tossed it through the remains of the back door. Even as the punishing blast of furnace-like high pressure washed over them, he grabbed Burke and towed him out of the building at speed.

"I'm not a fucking kite. Let me go or I'll bloody take off." Burke succeeded in freeing himself from the iron grip as they entered another building further down the block.

Rapid machine gun and automatic rifle fire came from somewhere in the front. The pair threaded their way through a maze of partitioned offices and dog-legging passageways. As Burke reached for a door-handle the firing abruptly ceased, there was a shout, a curse and then came the concussion of a grenade exploding. A fragment of casing came through the wood and passed between them to bury itself in a wall.

Before Burke could reach for the handle a second time the door swung open, revealing a scorched blood-streaked form, naked save for belt and boots. The bomb's victim took a staggering step forward, attempted to articulate, then vomited blood. As it crumpled, Dooley fired a burst past it at the Russian climbing in at the window. The brown-clad soldier was thrown back over the sill, his AKM falling into the room.

Another grenade followed immediately and they only just ducked back into the corridor in time. Dooley gave it a couple of seconds then replied with one of his own. The smoke cleared to reveal a Russian corpse laid on those of the Americans by the window . . .

"Let's try somewhere else. My choice this time." In fact it had to be his fifth, before Burke was able to lead Dooley into a small supermarket, sufficiently ahead of the approaching enemy infantry teams for them to catch their breath.

The respite was shortlived, a minute later Lieutenant Hogg appeared. He was armed with an AKM and trickles of blood from a scalp wound made red bars down his face.

"Get out of here you two. We've mined this place, we're going to sucker some commies into it."

Only then did Dooley notice the satchel charges beneath the shelves, and the wires trailing from them. "Shit, I like to watch the game, but not from the crappy in-field. We're with you, Lieutenant."

From the vantage point of the attic windows in the modest hotel that Hogg, with eleven other survivors, had turned into a stronghold, they had a good view of the front of the supermarket and of the rest of the street.

The roadblock was a hundred metres away, and the road between them and it was dotted with disabled or burning tanks and other armoured vehicles, six in all. But the rest of the column's tail had not driven into that killing ground, had held back, and now with the support of dismounted infantry was moving steadily forward, bringing massed firepower to bear on any opposition offered to its progress. Leading the advance was the T84 that had driven out Dooley and Burke. The tank's armour had been reinforced at all vulnerable points by additional welded-on plates, and every other area was festooned with water cans and toolboxes.

"That's going to be a bastard to stop." Burke examined the reinforced protection.

"Well have a good look at him, he won't be around for long."

The speaker was a launcher-toting signaller, with features so wrinkled and tanned he looked like an animated walnut. Burke made a slow, thorough inspection of him from head to toe and back again.

"If worry gave you a face like that . . ." he leant forward to read the name patch on the signaller's chest, ". . . York, then you're about to get a couple more lines to go with those you've got. That's if you can find the room for them."

"Funny man." York was not amused.

"Thanks. Compliments are always welcome." Turning his full attention back to the street, Burke saw that the T84 had pulled aside to allow a T72 bulldozer tank to pass. "With that tough bugger up front, looks like they're going to crash through."

An anti-tank rocket flashed from the entrance to an alley across the way, and struck the 'dozer tank on the big stowage bin fixed to the back of its turret. Tools and spare track links spun through the air. Almost before the crash of the detonation had died away, every enemy weapon sent shot or shell at the gap between the buildings.

Apparently unharmed by the hit, the awesome vehicle held its course for the roadblock, moving at an even walking pace. Its wide blade, held just above the surface of the road, collected odd pieces of furniture which it pushed before it until they broke up under the relentless pressure and passed beneath the bright leading edge, to be crushed by the tracks.

"Pick off a couple of the infantry when they're level with the supermarket." Keeping a tight grip on the remote detonator device, Hogg kept his teeth-exposing smile focused on the approaching enemy.

Two short bursts from Dooley's M16 sent the Russians diving for cover, leaving one of their number writhing on the ground. Giving them a moment to get right inside, the lieutenant flicked the switch. The delay lasted only a fraction of a second, but seemed an eternity, then all the glass burst from the store and, as flame followed, the whole fabric of the building disintegrated.

At that signal every weapon in the hotel opened up, and the street was hidden by the cloud of smoke and debris the torrent of fire kicked up.

"See that?" York threw down the empty launch tube and took up another. "I told you I'd get him."

"Better have another go." Burke saw the T84 drive into the open, and its cannon swing to bear on the hotel. "Those Ruskies aren't as impressed with your shooting as you are." There was what looked like a silver bead bordered dent in the tank's turret side. He knew those bright globules were the frozen runs of

125

molten metal, where the tank's sandwich filling of ceramic granules had defeated the shaped warhead, deflecting much of its effect before it could penetrate.

The mortar of the 'dozer tank had been damaged, as had one of the blade's arms, but it still moved inexorably toward the distant roadblock.

Lieutenant Hogg swore under his breath. Heck, he'd expected at least to knock out one of the damned things, but they still had tubes left, and the range was closing all the time. The M72s lacked the hefty punch of the Dragons, but a hit in the right place was just as fatal to any tank. He'd see them both burn yet. Strange, the T84 was holding its fire, maybe it had been damaged, a portion of the charge had penetrated; then he heard a sound from the floors below and knew why the enemy gunner was showing restraint.

The crack of the grenade's explosion had also been heard by Dooley. "Fuck that, the shitty Reds are in the building. Now we've got a fight." He took out his mirror-polished bayonet and clipped it in place. "Yeah, now we've got a real fight."

CHAPTER NINE

Hyde waited. He'd seen the building collapse after the Russian squad had entered, and the storm of fire unleashed on the tanks; and he knew that whatever the outcome of the fight further along the road, there would still be work left for him to do.

The Soviet armour was coming on fast now, and the volume of fire from the hotel had been reduced to sporadic bursts. Experience told him what was happening. The Reds were sacrificing their infantry to cover the tank's breakout, using bodies as shields for steel.

There had been no sound of fighting from the west side of the roadblock. If the head of the column had turned back, then Revell should have been engaging them by now. The silence from that direction was ominous. It meant that the bulk of the Soviet strike force was still racing, unchecked, for Frankfurt. He was glad it was Revell who'd have to pass that information on to Command, not him.

Now that the vehicles he'd already hit were

burning fiercely, most of the smoke was being driven straight up over the rooftops by the intense heat. Hyde had a clear view of the 'dozer tank as it drew nearer. He'd have to wait until it was side on, a frontal shot would be useless. The Dragon missile could pierce more than thirteen inches of metal, but with that great curved blade elevated it would be impossible for him to land a round directly on to the tank's front.

He settled against the sight, and became an extension of it as he waited for the T72 to enter his field of vision. The ground shook and the air was filled with the thunder of its V12 diesel engine as it accelerated.

A blur of mottled gray and green suddenly filled his sight. There was no time to take proper aim, the demolition tank would be past before he could. He hit the button, and sent the five and a half pound warhead on its way.

Reaction and flight time were only milliseconds, but the missile aimed at the tank's bow impacted beside its rear-drive sprocket, on the hull side just below the top run of track.

The tank's engine block burst through the deck behind the turret, and towing a coolant spouting radiator behind it, crashed into the road. Gushing flame, only its momentum kept the T72 going, but that was enough. Its forty-four tons smashed into the burning APC which formed half of the roadblock, tossing it aside, before veering to the left to follow its victim, and finally grinding to a halt against the side of the overturned and crushed-in hulk.

"Reload now." The shout came almost too late.

Dropping the rifle he'd taken up in order to pick off any escaping crewmen, Kurt was slow in supplying the fresh round. The closely following T84 was dashing for the gap even as Hyde clipped the fibreglass tube in place.

"Leave the crews for Clarence. We're after the bloody tanks." There was seething fury in his voice, but the portion of his mind operating the launcher stayed calm and detached. When he fired at the fast moving tank he made no mistake.

The exploding round broke a track and the tank slewed to a broadside stop, its bulk more than replacing the APC that had formerly obstructed the main street. Taking his time, Hyde put a second round into the base of its turret. The tank dissolved in a steel spawning fireball, peppering the buildings on either side with a hail of red-hot fragments.

"Reload. Damn you, give me a bloody reload." Hyde turned to lash out at Kurt, and checked himself.

The East German rocked on his heels, body shuddering, eyes bulging. He gesticulated, to elaborate on words that came out as no more than incoherent garglings. A jagged lump of track plate protruded from his chest.

Damn it, damn it, damn it. Revell had been about to fire at the T84 when Hyde's missile had stopped it. Now he was almost tempted to put a round into the hulk out of sheer frustration.

"They've gone, Major. Doesn't look like they're coming back." Boots scrunching on broken glass, Cohen re-entered through the back of the store.

129

"Must have decided to cut their losses."

"We've a third of their force bottled up. They've got to turn back." Staying locked to the sight, Revell willed another Russian crew to attempt a breakout, but there were no more. His only contact with the fighting raging on the far side of the successfully improvised barricade was the sound of the many weapons in action, and the stink and swirling smoke from the numerous fires.

"I reckon they didn't even stop to think about it, Major, just kept right on going. Twenty-plus commie wagons are still going like bats out of hell for Frankfurt." Taking off the borrowed binoculars Cohen offered them back, then when the officer made no move to accept them put them down beside him. "These are good, and I climbed up high as I could. If they were doing an about turn, I'd have known for sure. You want me to get through to Command?"

"Yes, get me a link." When he'd taken over the anti-tank weapon Revell had been sure, one hundred per cent certain, that the column's vanguard would return to rescue its severed tail, and it hadn't. He'd picked the hottest spot, and it had suddenly turned cold. The radio-man offered him the handset, he hesitated before accepting it. What the hell could he say . . .

". . . No. No we can't disengage and chase after it again . . . because my men are still dying here . . . Then if they're in place what the hell are you beefing about? . . . we've bought you all the time we can . . . the best part of half the job is done for you . . ."

Cohen listened anxiously, trying to figure out what was being said at the other end from Revell's

130

responses. Now why did the major always have to stick his neck out? Shit, it would take him forever to ingratiate himself with a new company commander, and that much longer to get his third stripe. Every time he thought things were lining up just right, something screwed it up. If Revell got the chop for insubordination ... Shit, and he'd been looking forward to making sergeant. Chances were Revell might make it first. Shit, shit, shit. That third stripe would have really helped him improve his profits.

With deliberate slowness, Revell replaced the handset. If he hadn't, he'd have slammed it down and probably broken it. He hated that, being chewed out by a staff officer, who was wetting himself a good hour before the forces he'd allocated even made contact with the enemy.

And the classy Boston accent got up his nose as well. Revell could imagine him: Old Family, Old Money, West Point and Staff College, with top marks and top people all the way. It would have been good to drag him out here, let him know real fear, facing the mindless ferocity of the Russians' sledgehammer tactics.

"So what now, Major?"

"The rest of the column is not our business anymore. They've got sky-spies tracking it and a reception is being arranged. We're to finish off here, so let's get on with it." With a last look at the flame-stained wall of steel still holding back the Russian rearguard, he folded the Dragon's tripod and picked it up, along with three reloads. "Bring what you can. We'll take these upstairs, see if we can still find a use for them."

A second-floor window gave them a view of the battle. The infantry fight seemed concentrated in the vicinity of a hotel further along on the far side of the street. As Revell watched, a squad of Russians sent several shoulder launched rockets into the ground floor, followed them with a flurry of grenades and then, hosing long bursts of automatic fire, charged inside.

Sporadic, and largely ineffective retaliation was coming from some upper windows, aimed mostly at the four armoured vehicles that were still in action.

Even as Revell aligned the sights on one, its hatches flew open and its crew scattered. Three rounds were required to ensure it was reduced to a condition that made re-manning out of the question.

Using a series of wrecks for cover, a pair of tanks made a move toward the roadblock. Before Revell could fire at the leader, a flame-tailed Dragon round lanced out from Hyde's location. It was a perfect shot, striking the base of the T84's turret immediately below its mantlet, but that was the extent of its success. Its fuse failed and it broke apart on impact like a frangible practice round. A few of the scattered lumps of explosive blazed fiercely on the road, some on the hull top, but the vehicle's fighting qualities were unimpaired.

For this very reason, the crew's behaviour seemed all the more incomprehensible. While the tank rolled on, they left its massively protected security and bolted in opposite directions.

To an unseen individual in the attic of the hotel the open hatches presented an irresistible attraction. One after another, four grenades were lobbed from the shutter-flanked garret. The last one bounced from the rim of the gunner's hatch and into the turret. There was no sound of an explosion, all that happened was that a large gray smoke-ring rose from the opening, but the effect on the tank was both immediate and dramatic.

Lurching, shuddering, it began to follow an erratic zigzag course toward the roadblock. Unguided save by whatever malfunction was affecting its steering, it succeeded in missing every major obstruction, riding over or thrusting aside any minor ones.

It was almost like being back on the ranges, and Revell waited until it was within seventy-five yards before sending the missile on its way. With instruction manual precision, the shaped warhead struck the base of the turret, which was ripped off by the resulting explosion.

"Still coming on, Major." Cohen could hardly believe it. With a tall pillar of fire gouting from the huge hole in its hull top, the unmanned target was maintaining its bizarre progress. "And I don't like the look of it."

"I'm not wasting a round . . ." Revell was already switching his aim to a Shilka flak-tank, that was trying to create a new side street by the brutal but effective process of crushing a picturesque half-timbered building.

"You'd better, Major. Its next turn will bring it right to us."

Revell couldn't achieve sufficient depression to bring the missile tube to bear on the new danger, and as he wrestled with the mount the burning tank clanked and squealed on to a heading that would bring it straight at them.

The masonry-topped hull of the embedded APC offered no real obstacle to the runaway. Without being deflected from its random course, the tank climbed the metal flank of the obstruction and, with its blow plate facing up to the sky and its steadily rotating tracks grinding great furrows in the carrier's armour, hung there for a moment.

Though he at last managed to fire, Revell knew it was useless. At so short a range the flight time was too brief for the missile to arm itself, and with only a fraction of its burn-out velocity, it broke into its component sections when it hit the target. Warhead, motor and electronics fell harmlessly onto the sidewalk amid a tangle of guidance wires.

There was just time for Cohen to snatch the radio pack and hunch over to protect it, before the APC's hull collapsed under the crushing weight, and the T84 was catapulted down and forward through the front of their building.

Flame from the explosive and diesel-fuelled fire swept up the stairs. Revell felt his throat constrict as rasping super-heated smoke filled the room, then was blinded by it as the floor began to sag and long, widening cracks raced up the walls.

The smoke was making it more difficult to find and identify targets. And there were fewer of them. Clarence repeatedly scanned the ground laid out below, but the only Russians to be seen were the dead and dying. When a group of survivers were occasionally forced to change position by the imminence of a building's collapse, they did so at the double, using every scrap of cover. Inevitably one of them would fail to make it, and the sniper would add another to his score, but only rarely was there the chance of a second shot.

Andrea was always ready when it happened. As the frantic infantry and dismounted tank crews piled in through another doorway, she would give them just a moment, then send a fragmentation grenade in after them. It was she who spotted the three officers attempting to set up a heavy machine gun in the car park behind the hotel.

"They are mine." She yanked on the sniper's arm as he took aim.

"We'll take them on together." Clarence pulled himself free.

"No, they are mine. This time it is you who will back me."

"Get on with it then." He couldn't keep the snap out of his words. This was the first time she'd asserted herself, and he didn't like it. So far they had worked perfectly as a team, until now she had accepted the role of giving support fire without question; in fact they'd reached the stage where few words were needed between them. It was as if a form of telepathy had joined their minds, making it possible for them to function as though they were one.

Taking the grenade from her depleted stock, Andrea didn't need to look as she dialled its fuse setting for an air-burst, and loaded it into the large bore tube below the rifle's barrel. The sniper's reaction to her demand had neither surprised nor bothered her; she had expected it. He could serve no further purpose, she had learnt all she could from him. It would take little to terminate their tenuous relationship. There had been nothing linking them beyond a shared interest in killing, and now there were other lessons to be learnt elsewhere—with another.

The 40mm grenade detonated right over the group, even as they brought the machine gun into action. Razor fragments scythed down from the gray smudge that banged into existence above the Soviet officers' heads.

There was anger in Clarence, mostly from old memories and more recent hatreds; but their recall had been triggered by Andrea's new air of dominance. It prompted him to do something he'd never purposely done before. One of the Russians hadn't gone down, he staggered about clutching at his stomach. The sniper carefully and deliberately put the 7.92mm bullet into the base of his spine.

At the impact the wounded man straightened up, arched backwards and flung his arms wide. A great mass of guts cascaded from the released wound, and the officer slipped in the dangling mess and fell to roll in them, before a final spasm sent his limbs into spastic jerks and he at last lay still.

Andrea had watched over the sights of her M16. A thin, tight smile turned up the corners of her beautiful mouth. "That was good. That was very good."

His thoughts were in a turmoil. There was so much he wanted to say, to explain, but he couldn't bring himself to speak to her. They might be fighting the same war, but they weren't fighting it the same way. Before, he'd felt they had much in common, now he knew that was an illusion. And he also knew, without having to ask again, the answer to the question he'd put earlier, and which she'd so consistently and expertly parried. She was in the war because she loved the killing.

Clarence watched her snap three fast single shots at a Russian sidling down a distant alleyway. Down to the stance and style, she had copied his technique to the last detail. It was as if, leech-like, she had sucked every single shred of knowledge from him. With single-minded determination she had spent hours on the ranges, and the result of all that practice, that honing of all she had absorbed from his unconscious instruction, had paid off. A body sprawled in an alley three hundred yards off testified to that.

"Who will it be next?" It was something he had to ask.

There was no hesitation, no surprise or mock confusion. "Perhaps the one who knows about heavy weapons, Libby. Or perhaps the big man, Dooley."

"Yes, you'll learn about fighting from him, and end up having to fight him off. Is that what you want? Or don't you mind so long as you pick up some useful tips on bayonet work?"

"Yes, I mind. But he will not touch me, I can look after myself. And if he should try, then I shall do something to him that will prevent his ever trying again."

Not for a moment did Clarence doubt her, she meant every word. Perhaps he was fortunate that his sex drive was dormant. Had he not been restrained by the crushing weight of his memories, it would have been very easy to feel strongly attracted to this superb young woman. Perhaps in time he would have been.

He looked at the scratch marks on the wall beside him. It needed just one more, just one to bring his score to two hundred. The opportunity came almost immediately. Only two blocks away, a Russian tank commander was hobbling down a side street. There was lots of time, even more when the target stopped to rest and rub a leg that a torn pair of coveralls revealed as livid and swollen. The powerful telescopic sight allowed him to see the man's face clearly as he grimaced from the pain of his wound.

Slowly and deliberately, Clarence aligned the cross-hairs on the man's thorax, at the base of his breastbone. A bullet there would do terrible damage, smashing ribs and driving them through the stomach and into most of the essential organs. Very gently, the sniper crooked his finger around the trigger. At the instant he exerted the slight pressure necessary, he jerked the tip of the barrel upwards.

Its velocity unimpeded by the padded helmet through which it first passed, the bullet stoved in the top of the Russian's head as he bent down. Coming out of the back of his neck, the now deformed round splattered hair and tissue and lumps of starred cranium across the wall on which he was leaning. The body slumped to a crouched position, head on knees, arms folded around them.

There was nothing special about number two hundred, nothing to mark the corpse as any different from the hundred and ninety-nine that had gone before, except that for a brief moment Clarence had come close to forgetting his real reason for doing it. Damn it, she had almost got to him. Well to hell with her, let her latch on to one of the others, he didn't need her. He didn't need anybody.

A movement in the graveyard caught his attention, and the faces of his children were before him as he took aim. He was remembering again, prepared to collect another payment.

CHAPTER TEN

"We can't just let him bleed to death." Ripper swabbed the deep red blood bubbling from the row of punctures in Wilson's chest with an already saturated field dressing.

Libby made a quick inspection of the ground-floor front lounge of the little house into which they had dragged the wounded man. With the exception of the locked door they'd kicked in to gain entry, it must have looked exactly the same as it did the day its owners had been forced to hurriedly abandon it. A large polished dresser appeared promising. Keeping low, and wedging the damaged door back into place as he passed it, he crossed the sculptured bronze-coloured carpet and tried each drawer in turn. From the third and fourth he took handfuls of napkins and a large white cotton tablecloth.

"Here," he tossed them to the young American, "use these. Bind them tight around his chest. It might help."

As Ripper stripped off the soaked jacket and shirt,

Libby went to the window, and standing back from it, using the cover of the partially drawn curtains, watched the Russians working to separate the truck from the carrier.

They had not bothered with a pursuit. Apart from posting a few nervous-looking machine gunners in various doorways, they seemed far more interested in getting mobile again. While they worked with sledgehammers and crowbars to part the entangled metal, the vehicle's turret constantly rotated to cover them with its heavy cannon.

With a final rain of massive blows, delivered by a hulking senior sergeant who had grabbed the hammer from a fast tiring private, the Russians were at last able to push the truck clear. A captain, who until now had not stooped to manual work, stepped forward and taking the implement from the sergeant, prodded the carrier's broken track.

"They're not going anywhere in a hurry." Leaving the window, Libby went to where Ripper had at last succeeded in fastening the improvised bandage. A huge white bow stood up on Wilson's chest, rapidly turning from pink to red, as it absorbed the continuing flow.

Wilson was unconscious. Each laboured breath brought another trickle of blood from the side of his mouth. The vivid streak running down his chin was in stark contrast with his pallor.

"What d'yer reckon. He gonna make it?"

"No." It was brutally abrupt, but Libby knew he'd be doing no favours by saying anything else, by holding out false hope. God only knew what had kept the Yank alive so far. He was hit in the lungs and must have lost the best part of four pints of blood already. It was everywhere, staining the carpet and Ripper and him.

"Aw shit. This weren't supposed to happen." Ripper made minor adjustments to the absurd bow, now losing its shape and collapsing as it blotted up more and more blood. "We only came out here for a spot of fun, to get a medal. What am I gonna tell his wife? He only got married just afore he came out here. Sally's expecting in the spring."

"You want to tell her anything you better concentrate on keeping yourself alive, that's unless you want to end up like him." It wasn't the casualty on the floor Libby was referring to. He jerked his thumb toward the scene of the collision. "Did you know him as well?"

Not taking his eyes off his friend, Ripper shook his head. "First time I seen him was today. They gonna do that to Wilson as well?"

It always came as a shock to the new men, the first time they saw the treatment meted out by the Russians to the bodies of NATO troops. Libby had seen it too often to still be deeply affected, but now and again some communist NCO or officer would come up with a new idea, and then the atrocities listed against the Warsaw Pact forces would be lengthened by yet another degrading obscenity.

The body of the truck's driver had been extricated from the crushed metal of the cab, and a couple of Russians, directed by the hammer-wielding senior sergeant, had roughly nailed it to a door before

143

dousing it in fuel and setting it alight.

Now the corpse's bullet-shattered head drooped to contemplate with empty soot-filled sockets the charred ruin of its body. Close-by, the APC's crew worked on their damaged track, apparently oblivious to the appalling stench.

"If they find him, I expect they'll make the time. They don't ever get leave, or much free time come to that, so they look on it as a sort of entertainment, light relief. That's nothing to what they get up to if they get hold of our wounded."

"That's sick. Hell, where I'm from we got some real mean guys. The sort of fellas who'd stamp you into the ground, then come back and sue yer for damaging their boots, but that lot out there, they're sick. I heard the stories, but that . . ."

"That's nothing." Libby got out another table-cloth and pulled dust sheets off the furniture to make blankets. A spasmodic shaking gripped the wounded man and his hands and forearms were cold to the touch. He draped them over him, tucking them in about his chin.

"Ever since the revolution, they've been doing a bugger sight worse things to their own people. How many did Stalin get through, twenty million? And how many was it that Brezhnev starved in the labour camps, or had tortured in the Lubianca, or turned into cabbages by sticking them in mental wards and pumping them full of drugs? The civies back home think they're such a fucking clever crowd, keeping the war in the Zone. All they're bloody doing is giv-ing the commies more time to practise. If they gave us

144

the weapons and the men to do the job once and for all, we could shove them all the way to bloody Siberia, and back into the fucking dark ages."

"Seems to me as some of them reckon they're still there."

"They are." Slowly and carefully, Libby slid another cushion beneath Wilson's head as pink bubbles formed at his nostrils. "The commies are at about the same level as the Japs were at the start of World War Two, and you know what they got up to."

"He feels awful cold."

Libby moved Ripper's hand, and felt for a pulse. It was hard to find, weak and fluttery. "Not long now. Better get ready to move out. Sounds like there's still plenty of fighting going on in the centre of town."

"I'm not leaving him, no way." There was aggression in Ripper's abrupt announcement.

"That wasn't what I said . . ." The bubbles had stopped growing and popping at Wilson's nostrils. Libby sought the pulse again. ". . . but there's no point in staying now. He's gone."

"Give me a grenade." Ripper held out his hand.

"Are you thinking of doing something silly?" Without giving it a second thought, Libby had reached for one of the fragmentation grenades attached to his webbing. He paused, and didn't unclip it.

"I'm gonna get me a commie battle taxi. I owe it."

The long thin bony fingers were still held out toward him, making opening and closing grasping gestures. "You can't take out an APC with one of

145

these. The best you'll manage is to stir up a bloody hornet's nest."

"OK, so tell me how I do it then." He'd withdrawn his hand and was now stripping Wilson's body of its spare ammunition. "I reckon it'd please him if I used some of his lead for this job. That'd be a kinda justice, don't you think?"

"I suppose so. Alright, we'll do it together, but we do it my way." Libby handed over two grenades. "You remember that. My way."

"Don't matter a cuss to me which way, so long as it gets done." Before standing up, Ripper removed Wilson's dogtags. They were wet and sticky with congealed blood. "I sure do wish I could take him home to Sally, for a decent Christian burial. Don't seem right, leaving him here, like this."

"You can tell graves registration. Make a note of the address, otherwise he might lay here for years. They'll take care of him. He'll have a proper burial, eventually."

"Yeah, I'll do that." Ripper flicked the edge of a dust sheet over the pale face. "Now how about we go kill ourselves a whole parcel of commies?"

All the houses on the road had been locked, a symbol of the touchingly hopeful faith of the town's fleeing inhabitants in the possibility of returning one day. It was difficult to quietly gain access to one close by the scene of the collision, and when they at last resorted to breaking a pane of glass, the sound of its falling onto a tiled kitchen floor seemed monstrously loud, coming as it did during a short lull in the battle.

There was a smell of decay in the house, strongest near the expensive fitted units in the kitchen. Green mould filled the shelves of an open fridge and spread across the floor, following the course the melted ice had taken. On a worktop, there was evidence that a meal had been in the midst of preparation when the alert had sounded.

"You looking for something?" Expecting to head straight for the front of the building, Ripper couldn't work out what was going on, when Libby lingered in the kitchen to rake and rummage through every cupboard.

Stuffing an assortment of clinking bottles and various garish plastic containers into a pedal bin liner he hastily emptied of stale rubbish, Libby ignored the question, then led his companion at a fast pace through the dining room and lounge and up the stairs to the top floor. They barely made it in time.

Some of the Russians had begun to take an interest in the contents of the houses about them, and one after another front doors were collapsing before determined shoulder charges.

"Better get ready. They could try here soon." Taking one of the containers from the bag, Libby ripped a sheet into strips and began to bind a grenade to it. "Give me a hand then." He pushed a selection across the double bed to Ripper.

"Now what's this supposed to do?" Ripper examined the label on a two litre bottle of lavatory cleaner, an illustration making its application obvious. "You want to make them clean round the bend?"

"Funny, ha, ha. Just bloody do it." Finishing the first, Libby picked up a bottle of bleach and gave that similar treatment. "I'm fed up with being on the receiving end of that chemical muck the Ruskies are forever chucking about, it's our turn to have a go with the stuff. Or at least make the buggers think we are. Soon as they catch a whiff of this, you watch them panic." Cautiously, he moved to the window.

The Russians were beginning to emerge with their booty from the houses they had already looted. As they sorted it, deciding what to keep and what to abandon, their decisions were frequently peculiar, prompted more by whether or not it was possible to get a particular object aboard their transport than by the value of the article.

Their officer strolled about with an affected attitude of disinterest, but now and again he would pounce on one of the piles and appropriate some piece for himself, handing them to a private staggering along in his wake, burdened with a bulging valise.

As a pair of junior sergeants approached the house, there came a shout from the men working on the damaged track. They had completed the repairs. With their officer deeply occupied with gaining a larger than fair share of the strangely assorted loot, the enemy machine gun teams began a hasty and incautious withdrawal back to the APC.

"There won't be a better chance than this." Libby took a grenade and attached bleach container, and pulled out the pin. "Lose that window when I tell you."

Down below, spurred on by the continuing sounds of bitter fighting from elsewhere in the town, the Russians were forgetting rank and manners as they made a crush at the carrier's rear doors.

"Now!"

Twenty rounds from Ripper's assault rifle shattered the still rain-dotted panes and broke apart the peeling frames. Through the hail of spinning fragments the ill-balanced contrivance tumbled end over end. It struck the road a few yards short of the carrier and went off immediately in a great cloud of steam and spray.

The sudden and overpowering stench sent the Russians into a panic as it washed over them. The scramble to get into the carrier ceased abruptly and every man snatched frantically at the pouch holding his respirator, elbowing others aside to lift it to his face.

A fight broke out as a soldier without his mask tried to snatch another's. The struggle was short and violent and the respirator's new owner stood on his victim's body to put it on.

The deception was reinforced by two more of the devices. Both exploded in the air, sending a drenching cloud of pungent household chemicals toward the Russians. At that their nerve broke, those already aboard slammed the doors on the men still trying to get in, and the APC began to lurch through an ill-judged turn that brought it into collision with several houses in turn. The succession of jarring impacts gave its turret gunner no chance to bring his weapons to bear, and as the carrier completed the manoeuvre it passed right under Libby's window.

Concentrating on bringing down the last of the abandoned infantry, Ripper only caught a glimpse of the bundle of grenades Libby tossed out. He brought up his rifle after fitting a fresh magazine, and leveled it at an officer who appeared hesitant, uncertain whether to seek cover, or chase after his vehicle. A group of five bullets aimed at the Russian's chest went wildly astray as Ripper was bowled over by a heavy tackle about his knees.

"What are you up to? You made me miss the bastard."

"Keep your bloody head down." Cradling his head on his arms, and opening his mouth wide Libby waited for the blast. The air was thick with the fumes of diesel exhaust and bleach, then it was broiling hot as well, as a huge shock caught the building and shook it. First the floor slammed up into them, then as a fireball passed the windows the walls shed great slabs of plaster and the ceiling fell in. It became almost impossible to breathe in the choking dust that reduced visibility virtually to nil.

"Jesus, what was that, you got some pocket-size nukes?" Dazed, spitting out dust and pieces of carpet pile, Ripper needed the support of an overturned coffee table as he got shakily to his feet. "Hey, those commies ain't the only ones who play for keeps." He stuck his head out of the window. At first glance the APC, now immobile with its motor still running raggedly, hadn't been all that badly damaged. Most of the force of the blast had been borne by the hull top, just to the rear of the turret. But as he looked harder he could see strips of rubber beading hanging down the armoured side of the vehicle. They came from the bottom rim of the turret, now lifted off its ring. There were dents and buckles in the roof of the carrier and it had been holed in several places.

Some of the bodies lying about had been caught by the devastating blast and were piled grotesquely together in a small front garden. Chunks of flesh decorated leafless trees, an arm had come to rest in a window box.

"Stick your stupid head out like that and you're liable to get it shot off." Libby was about to drag his companion back inside, when the carrier's nearside rear door slowly began to open. "I thought I'd got them all." He watched, the squeal from the grating metal of the distorted hinges making him clench his teeth.

The door opened a little way, and after a pause a light coloured cloth was flapped from it. Blood-stained fingers were just visible clutching a corner, and the movements were weak.

"No, let's wait and see. Even if it's a trick, we'll be better off with them out in the open." It had taken an effort on Libby's part not to fire. Almost from the first days of the war, the NATO troops had learnt never to trust the offer of surrender by Russians. Time and time again they had used it as a ploy to gain an advantage, and now Libby never bothered to even consider if a capitulation was genuine. He'd seen too many good men die while they took time to give it thought, tricked into dropping their guard for an instant.

After a moment the gesture was repeated, and then the door began to open further. Another pause, and then three badly wounded men crawled and stumbled from the APC's dark interior. The first could hardly stand, in his right hand he held the makeshift flag, with his left he supported the smashed remnant of his bottom jaw. The two who followed were in a worse condition, and bled from several penetrating wounds of the head, chest and thighs, where they had been caught while sitting down, by the overhead burst. They moved slowly away from the APC, until they came to the centre of the road, then stopped and, like cattle uncertain of a reprieve from slaughter, stood or sat as they were able, waiting for the initiative to come from elsewhere.

Ripper was all set to fire, had his finger on the trigger, but held back. "You know, I kinda hate wasting good bullets on them. If I had a dog in that sort of state back home, I'd finish it with a length off the woodpile."

"That's one of their tricks, among others. One way and another the medics get saved a lot of work in the Zone."

"What'd yer think then, do I finish them, or do you want first go? I'm easy."

"Leave them." That surprised Libby himself, those weren't the words he'd meant to say. He rationalised it. "They'll not last long, leave them to bleed. Like you say, why waste bullets." Not since they'd discovered the enemy were using dum-dum and explosive bullets had Libby knowingly spared a Russian, and even before that there had been few occasions. The fighting was always too fierce, too fast moving to admit the taking of prisoners. There was no certainty about those three succumbing to their injuries, terrible though they obviously were, but still he didn't fire. Oh what the hell, let them go, they'd be taking no more part in the battle. Maybe he was beginning to have had enough of killing. It was a certainty he'd stop the moment he found Helga, and it would be without any regret, without any guilt either. Two years fighting the Warsaw Pact Forces in the Zone had taught him to expect no quarter, and he in turn had given none. But those three out there, they no longer presented any threat, so what was the point? Let them live, at least the few minutes they had left. He was doing them no favours, judging by the state they were in; yes, let them live. He put his hand out to push down the barrel of Ripper's M16.

The rattle of the rapid automatic fire went on a long time and echoed all about the street. Each of them hit by several rounds, the wounded Russians jerked and rolled and doubled-up.

"From over there." It was Ripper who had pinpointed the spot from which the firing had come. His bullets smacked dust from the doorway, but the Russian officer had already ducked back out of sight.

There were three more dead in the road. One of them still clutched a large pale piece of cloth, now spattered with his own blood and soaking up more that flowed about it. Puddles turned red as they mingled the separate streams coming from the bodies.

"That guy killed some of his own. What'd he do that for?"

153

"Could be any of a dozen reasons." Libby started out of the room, talking back to Ripper over his shoulder as he followed. "Most likely reason is fear. The same thing that's driving that column on. A Soviet officer can lose ninety, a hundred per cent of his men in battle and so long as the objective is achieved, who cares, sure as hell his superiors won't, all they want is results." He led the way out through the kitchen. "But let the same poor bugger have a single man desert and God help him. So, when they have to, they prevent their men from going over the hill, or surrendering or changing sides by ways like you just saw. As a system it works, and it suits the commie mentality. If they can't terrify a poor sod into blind obedience, they kill him. Bang, no problem."

"They sure ain't too nice, not by half."

"You haven't seen anything yet." Checking each alleyway and side street they had to cross with extreme caution, Libby led as they worked their way toward the main street. "The real beauties are the party officials, the ones with GLAVPUR, the Red Army's political directorate. Now those specimens really know all about being nasty. If we get out of this, go and see one of the POW cages where they're kept, you'll find it an education."

"Kinda seems like that's what I'm getting at the moment." Ripper covered the Britisher as he sprinted across the corner of a small square, then followed as soon as Libby had taken up a position to cover him in turn.

"No, this is just a pre-school playgroup, kinder-garten. Wait until you get to college, one of the big set piece scraps with nukes and all."

They were getting close to the scene of the fiercest fighting. Overlapping waves of suppressed air from grenade and shell explosions made Ripper's ears pop, and brought cordite-heavy smoke to bite into his throat and lungs. His eyes began to water. "I can wait, all of a sudden I ain't chasing medals no more."

CHAPTER ELEVEN

The bayonet was stuck fast, gripped by the ribs between which it had penetrated. Shit, he'd been thrusting for the gut. Dooley could tell from the commie's slack-jawed glazed expression, and from the increasing downward drag on his rifle that a second blow wasn't needed, but his immediate problem was freeing the M16. He braced himself against the inevitable recoil, and fired.

Its muzzle rammed hard against the Russian, the weapon's kick was vicious. Prepared though he was, Dooley's arm was momentarily numbed as the bayonet withdrew.

A whistling sigh escaped the blade's victim, cut short as the big man's boot crushed his kneecap and sent him tumbling down the stairs. It was a body that hit the landing below, almost falling on another Russian who was making ready to hurl a grenade. The snap shot that Dooley followed up with didn't hit him, but whined past the grenadier, close enough to startle him and cause him to hold on to the bomb a fraction too long.

"Hey, that was an own goal, how about that?" Dooley realised that the celebration might have been a little premature when a long burst of machine gun fire came up through the boards beside him, and slivers of wood lanced into his calf. "Fuck that. Ain't you broken through that wall yet?" There was no answer. He backed up a few paces along the corridor, and another crackle of fire came through precisely where he'd been standing. "Come on, it can't be taking you that long. If they can shove stuff up through the floors, you must be able to get through to next door."

Lieutenant Hogg came down from the staff quarters. "Things getting too hot for you?"

"I ain't chucking my life away while Cohen could be out cold and cashable." A grenade bobbed over the top of the stairs and rolled to Dooley's feet. Without hesitation he reversed his rifle and, using it like a five-iron, sent it back. "Fuck this, they're beginning to cheese me off." He took a blast grenade of his own, and tossed it after the other.

Coming almost together, the detonations shook the building and as a wall of dust rushed at Hogg, he became aware of a new noise. It grew louder, a splintering tearing sound. He grabbed Dooley and pulled him back as the stairs and several yards of the corridor vanished, raising still further clouds of dust as they crashed to the floors below. A strong smell of burning came to their noses, and with it the groans and shouts of trapped men.

"Did you mean to do that?"

"Of course I did."

158

Disbelief shaded Hogg's expression, but he said nothing further as they made their way to the attic rooms.

"How's that?" York stood by an irregular hole hacked in the gable end. "I said I'd make a good job." The praise he'd been expecting didn't materialise. "Well I reckon it's a good job."

"All we want is a way out, not a triumphal arch." Burke and a two man machine gun team went first.

Hogg supervised the departure of the others. The roof space had filled with smoke, and the floor was growing hot as he made a last check.

The adjoining property was one floor lower, and there was a ten foot drop to its steeply pitched tiled roof. Dooley and a couple of others had already set to work smashing an entrance through it.

"Here, let me have a go, I'll show you." Attacking the growing opening enthusiastically, York smashed his rifle butt up and down, sending shards of gray tile skittering off the roof on to the road below. "Just once more." Raising the weapon above his head, he brought it down with pile-driver force. It missed and went straight through the hole, and York went with it.

"Jesus, he'll do anything for a laugh." Dooley went next, exercising more caution and making a feet first landing on the bed that had broken York's fall.

"You damned near landed on my head." There were several cuts on York's face.

"With a head that size, I'd have had trouble avoiding it wherever I fucking landed."

Machine gun fire from the street was breaking tiles as the last man swung in the hole for a moment before dropping down, then his brains showered over everybody and he plummetted to the floor sickeningly hard. There was no need for anyone to check, the top of his head had been shot off.

Lieutenant Hogg shouldered his AKM, and took the rocket launcher from beneath the body. "OK, so what are we waiting for. Come on, the Reds know we're in here, do you want to fight your way out of here as well?"

A tank shell passed through the room a moment after they left and another shower of powdered plaster chased them down the stairs. Letting the rest of the men pass, Hogg ducked into a small front room and crossed to the window. On the far side of the street a T84 had its main gun trained on the building. The nearest turret hatch was open, and a crewman was using the anti-aircraft machine gun to hose long bursts at every window in turn. Hogg just had time to duck when one of the fusillades came his way. Incendiary rounds lodged in the walls, window frame and furniture and began to give off white smoke as their phosphorus content ignited.

It was the first time Hogg had ever used one of the M72 launchers, except for a dummy during basic training. Now he prayed he'd remembered all he'd been told. The safety pins securing the waterproof end seals came out easily, and he gingerly extended the telescopic launch tube to cock the firing mechanism. Supporting the front end with his left hand, the back of the tube on his shoulder, he approached the window again. His right hand played over the top of the launcher, seeking the trigger button. He found it, and his index finger rested lightly on it as he aligned the flip-up sights.

This was what he'd been waiting for, the chance to dish out a bit of what he'd been on the receiving end of for a year. How many times had he watched truckloads of infantry driving over the bridges he'd built, and wished he was going with them as he saw the cluster of improvised crosses in a nearby plot? How many times had he and his company of combat engineers dug in around the approaches to one of their fabrications, waiting for an enemy attack that never came? It had always been the other companies that'd had the heroic struggles. Well if the mountain wouldn't come to him . . .

"Aim for the base of the turret."

Taking Burke's advice, Hogg shifted his point of aim. "Why haven't you got out with the others?"

"For a start I can't stand that bloke York, and I reckon if I'm going to be lumbered with having to do a bit of the swash and buckle lark, I might as well do it in front of an officer and make sure I get a gong."

Detecting an unexpected ring of truth in the answer, Hogg didn't pursue it any further. He held his breath, gently increased the pressure of his grip, and then felt the heat of the rocket's blast on his back.

A flurry of smoke which quickly drifted clear was all that marked the hit. Hogg felt disappointed, he had hoped for something altogether more impressive and spectacular. He hadn't even scratched it.

"Nice one, Lieutenant, you sure you haven't done this before?"

At Burke's compliment Hogg took a second look. The T84 still looked the same . . . or did it? There was no sign of the machine gunner, and gray exhaust no longer blew from the vehicle's rear. Then he noticed a tiny flicker of flame coming from the turret hatch. It grew as he watched until it was a swirling pillar of orange and yellow, reaching past the tops of the buildings, as though the tank had begun to consume itself in its moment of death. The driver's hatch flew open and another spiralling tongue grew. "Hey, I got it. Will you look? I got it."

"If we don't get out of here he'll have got us." A stamp of his boot, and Burke temporarily checked the advancing small curling flames licking along the edge of the carpet.

"I really got it." Hogg was hardly conscious of Burke propelling him from the room, past the blazing furniture and down the stairs. He felt elated. He'd done it, he'd done it. This must be how a fighter pilot felt at his first kill. It made up for all the mud the commie shells had shovelled over him, all the times they had forced him on to his face and pummelled his body with series of concussions. "I got a tank."

"Great." The tone Burke used conveyed no enthusiasm. "That's just great. That leaves about seventeen thousand still to go."

Hogg stopped his repetitive chant. "OK, let's go find them."

"Don't be in such a hurry, Lieutenant. You can save a lot of energy by waiting right where you are. It's the Ruskies who come looking for us."

Horrible bubbling noises were coming from Kurt's chest as air found its way into his body cavities, past

162

the deeply embedded fragment. Fighting the pain, his face contorted in ugly grimaces, his head lolled from side to side, and there was a constant trickle of blood from the side of his mouth. But still the Grepo clung to life, even hauling himself to a sitting position in the dark corner where Hyde had dumped him. A trail of blood marked where he had been dragged.

With both lungs damaged, Hyde hadn't expected him to last more than a minute. He was drowning in his own blood and the smashed ribs and breastbone must have been agony, so why hang on, why fight it?

Hyde knew what it was like to hurt that bad. He'd made an attempt to kill himself before the pain and the shock of his burns had made him unconscious. And when he'd come round it had been worse, and when the suffering had become so great he thought it could only get less, they had started the grafts. Month after month, piece by piece, they had given him back something that would pass for a face. The new eyelids had been the worst. After the first stage of rebuilding those he'd almost tried to take his own life again, and Kurt was hanging on in spite of something as bad as that . . .

"*Wasser, wasser.*"

It was a temptation to ignore the plea for water, pretend he hadn't heard the faint words that came with pink foam from Kurt's mouth. But he didn't. Leaving the Dragon, Hyde took his water bottle over.

"No, don't bloody gulp it. I said don't . . . Just a sip, a bloody sip." The urge to hit Kurt was almost overwhelming. It was something Hyde had always wanted to do, and now the constantly clutching and

163

clawing greedy hands wore at his patience, and he nearly did.

With a final wrench he pulled the bottle away. It was sticky with blood. "Here, have the bloody lot if you want." Hyde thrust it back at the East German. "Go on, kill your ruddy self. Do us all a great big favour."

Through the pain Kurt heard the words, and with a weak fling of his arm knocked the water from Hyde's grasp, sending it clattering and bouncing to spill behind an overturned counter and irrigate the draught-drifted dust.

"Playing the tough bastard are you, reckon you're going to make it?" Hyde stuck his face close to the wounded man's. "Now why should a piece of shit like you pull through, when a load of decent blokes never do? Have you seen the hole you got in your gut? It's as big as that." He held his fist in front of Kurt. "I can see your lungs, what's left of them. You're not going to make it, so why try?"

He tried hard, but Kurt couldn't manage to articulate again. Instead he made a familiar gesture with two fingers of his right hand. Blood ran down into his sleeve as he did so.

Once again, Hyde had to fight down the desire to hit out. He knew if he stayed there he would, and forced himself back to the Dragon. There was no target in sight on which he could vent his feelings. Every one of the dozen armoured vehicles littering the street was either burning or severely damaged, and there was nothing to be seen of their crews, save for a few smouldering and dismembered bodies scattered about at random. Fighting was still going

164

on further along the street, in the vicinity of the hotel, but the hazy atmosphere made it impossible for him to be certain of any of the fleeting targets he glimpsed.

The machine gun upstairs still chattered intermittently, sending tracer zipping away into the smoke, but at what and with what effect Hyde couldn't tell. That was one of the crazier aspects of war in the Zone. Even now, with all the modern communication aids available, even in the midst of a great set piece battle that might involve whole armies of men, it was still possible to be alone, feel totally isolated. It was eerie to hear the conflict raging all around, occasionally glimpse some part of it and yet to be completely cut off from what was happening. All you could do was kill, and keep on killing in the hope that enough of your side were doing the same to gain a victory. Not that there were many of those in the Zone.

A mass attack by Russian divisions would be met with a stubborn NATO defence. There'd be breakthroughs, local counteroffensives, withdrawals to previously prepared positions, spoiling attacks, raids . . . a whole alphabet of jargon phrases would be trotted out for the media and for "morale." And all too often the end result was a further widening of the Zone, a million more refugees, fifty thousand dead, a couple more points on the radiation scale and both sides claiming victory.

This was a stinking little scrap. Messy, probably costly by now. No medals, no headlines, but maybe a few days' leave, with luck. Not that he ever went far from the Zone. The civies who lived with it on their doorstep were more tolerant of the freaks and monsters it produced, like him. And there were women too, who were used to the rough usage of camp followers. Last time he'd even found one who'd taken his money and performed with him while sober. Usually he had to wait until late, find a drunken prostitute and get her into a dark alley; and even then pray she wouldn't see his face by the light of a match or passing headlights. But it had been good the last time, good by the standards he had to accept.

God, he had to admit it, she'd been ugly. Not just plain, but really ugly. To a face pockmarked by acne had been added the embellishment of a long razor scar. And she was fat, not obese, but well beyond plump and she'd smelt of cheap perfume, sweat and stale tobacco; for all that he'd enjoyed her.

The flat she'd taken him to matched her perfectly, mostly scruffy, the few decent pieces in garish bad taste. By then he'd been in a hurry, two months of enforced celibacy and a huge erection urging him on. Following her into the tiny bedroom, he'd switched off the light and grabbed her as she started to undress.

Two giant breasts had filled his hands and his fingers had sought the nipples to knead them to hardness. She'd tried to break free, to remove the rest of her clothes, but he hadn't been able to wait, had pushed her face down onto the bed. He had thrown her skirt up over her back, then grabbed the waist of the tights and knickers and tugged them down together, frantically fast.

Forcing her legs wide apart, he'd knelt between

166

them and released his erection. For an instant he'd held it in his hand. The pale light filtering into the room through threadbare curtains revealed enough for him to savour the moment. His hot flesh reaching well out beyond his tightly clenched hand, the big twin mounds of her backside, and the long dark crevasse between them; the deep indent left by her bra strap, just visible above the bunched-up material of her skirt. He had forced one other delay on himself, lowering his body until the hard rod of muscle lay between the cool smooth hummocks of fat.

Then he'd felt himself beginning to pulsate and he'd slid down to bring its tip into her bush of pubic hair. At the fourth hard prod she'd complained, fractionally lifted her belly from the bed, and slid a hand down to her crotch. Questing fingers had sought and found him, guiding his moisture-crowned penis inside her.

The memory of that never-ending orgasm was still with him. It had seemed as though the sperm was going to pump from him forever. Beneath him, the fat legs had clamped together, trapping his body inside her and, as she fingered herself from the front, her hips had gyrated wildly and she'd matched his experience with a climax that had soaked them both. They'd coupled twice more, and between each one she'd encouraged him to use a vibrator on her, and in return she'd gone down on him and sucked him to new hardness.

Hyde removed an anti-tank round from the Dragon and replaced it with one fitted with an anti-personnel fragmentation warhead. There were infantry moving about on the other side of the road. Smoke from burning buildings made it difficult to identify them. He switched the sight-unit to infra-red, then held his fire as he recognised the distinctive weapons and helmets of NATO troops.

So it was nearly over, mopping-up had begun. It wouldn't do any harm to sit tight a little longer, just in case some Reds had decided to play dead for a while and were now thinking of springing a surprise. If that happened, then by not giving his position away he'd be able to catch them at their own game.

And besides, there was still Kurt, he'd need help shifting him. How on earth the Grepo was hanging on to life was a mystery, but he was, and showed no sign of letting go. It would have been easy for Hyde to take advantage of the situation and finish him off. God knew the runt had enough ugly crimes against his name to warrant summary execution, but that wasn't his way. But if he wouldn't kill Kurt, there was no reason why he should help keep him alive. Maybe he'd take his time about getting help, he could square that with himself easily enough.

Sporadic shooting was still to be heard, but no more heavy calibre weapons were in action. How many would there still be at the final roll-call? Not many of that green mob the officer of engineers had brought with him, that was for certain. Clarence would come through, he always did, he was one of the great indestructibles, seemingly a permanent feature of the Zone. Even the Russians had found out about him somehow, and had posted a reward for his capture. The others, probably, but the fighting had been close and bloody, not all the advantages in the world could have entirely made up for the disparity in fire-power between themselves and the section of the column they had cut off and carved up.

And it wasn't only the Russian armour that had taken a beating. Further along, a large flame-enveloped building suddenly bowed outwards, sagged and collapsed across the road, partially burying a disabled self-propelled gun. Other shops and houses were beginning to burn, whole blocks in some cases. A few premises had already been reduced to heaps of smouldering rubble. The centre of the town had been gutted and the devastation would be spread over a larger area by the unchecked fires.

One of the machine gun team came clattering down the stairs. Hyde noted that the only sign of the mass of ammunition they had carried up was the short length of belt actually hanging from the M60 he had over his shoulder. "Where's the other one?"

"Tracer round from that flak-wagon got him. Cut him in half." The machine gunner brushed a length of intestine from his boot. "I didn't even know he'd bought it until I called for another belt, and all of a sudden he wasn't there. Will your guy make it?" He bent over Kurt and reached out to touch the lodged fragment, then stopped when the wounded man raised his M16 to point it, waveringly, alternately at his chest and throat. "OK fella, if that's the way you want it."

He joined Hyde by the window. "You sure that guy's on our side?"

"Well he is, but I've never been sure of it. He's ex-

169

border guard." Hyde offered the American a boiled sweet.

"Thanks, don't mind if I do." He sucked loudly. "Can't say I'm too fond of those creeps. He's hurt so bad, I don't suppose there's any real hurry."

"No, none at all." Sergeant Hyde offered the bag again. "I think we've got time for another."

The Zone - Southern Sector

In a concentrated weekend of action, Yugoslav regular and irregular forces have succeeded in closing virtually every airport being used by the Russian Airforce. Sixteen fighters, forty helicopters and thirty-seven transport aircraft were destroyed on the ground. The action was timed to coincide with the closing of the Vardar Valley, and the destruction of the main road/rail links with Bulgaria by irregular forces supported by air-strikes provided by US 6th Fleet, Mediterranean.

Warsaw Pact Forces inside the country are being forced to feed themselves off the land, and there have been several clashes between farmers and foraging Bulgarian troops. Six civilians died in one incident.

The World Council of Neutral Nations has again called on Russia and Hungary to remove their troops from Austria.

*   *   *

Switzerland has admitted responsibility for the shooting down of the C-141 Starlifter of 55th US Aeromedical Airlift Squadron. The aircraft came down near Andelfingen, on Euroroute 70. The crew and fifteen medical attendants, plus all seventy-five litter cases from the 27th US Division were killed in the crash. No explanation has been offered.

Switzerland has complained of harassment and physical assault on its nationals in several German cities, and demanded compensation for the burning of the Consulate in Munich by American Forces personnel.

CHAPTER TWELVE

The respirator helped. Its filters had been designed to keep out microparticles of toxic chemicals, and now they reduced the amount of smoke Revell was forced to take in with each painfully laboured breath. Flame gushed up the stairs, gouted through every crack in the floorboards. He felt the heat strike at him, so fiercely that every movement which brought his clothes into fresh contact with his body was a moment of pain.

Cohen was still holding the radio pack. Now he found Revell's arm, and too hoarse to use the mask's short-range built-in radio, urgently signalled to the upper floors. He repeated the gesture as Revell shook his head.

"No good, no good." Fumes bit into the major's throat and reduced him to cryptic abbreviations of what he wanted to say. "The back, the back."

Part of the front wall fell away, and was replaced by a sheet of flame. Revell didn't waste more time on words, shoving Cohen toward the rear of the building. To reach it, they had to skirt the roaring jet coming up from the furnace below. As they drew level with it the air became unbreathable, and plucked at them, sucking them toward the yellow and red inferno streaming to the top of the building.

Hell was below them, all about them, and Revell could only see Hyde's ghastly parody of a face wherever he looked. Better to get it over with quick, then cling to life like that.

Then they were past, and heard the room they had left thunder down on top of the burning tank. Now fire curled along the ceiling as well, pushing rolling black clouds ahead of it. Light fittings and ceiling tiles caught and dripped fire onto them, falling with rippling zipping sounds, like vertical streaks of miniature tracer.

Bars blocked the window and the vision of Hyde returned. Revell sought another way. His fingers made contact with a metal bar. A fire door . . . it had to be. He ran his hand around the edge of the steel panel until he found the bolts he'd been expecting.

Had to stay calm, that was it, stay calm. Damn, that hurt. A blob of something molten struck the back of his hand. He could feel the pressure of the radio-man's grip on the sleeve of his jacket.

"It's OK, found a door, out in a minute." He shouldered his repeater 12-gauge and tried the release bar. The door remained stubbornly shut. Oh God, don't let it be warped, or rusted or jammed by expansion in this heat. Another attempt, and all he managed was to skin his knuckles. He didn't dare to turn and look at the flames he knew would be there.

Think, he had to think, had to force himself to

174

slow down, rationalise. Two bolts, he'd done them. The locking bar itself, he'd tried that every way. He was being stupid, it had to open, damn it, it had to. Again he pulled with all his strength, and the door didn't budge an inch. It must be something basic. This was crazy. As a kid he'd never had any trouble opening the emergency doors to let his friends in for free . . . Once more he took hold of the handle, lifted it until he heard the "clunk" of the lock disengaging, and pushed. The door swung gently open and, with Cohen in tow, he tumbled out on to the fire escape.

Tearing off his respirator, he gulped in fresh air. Tears still flooded his eyes and blurred his vision. When he started down and reached for the railing he missed it and slipped the first few steps, skinning the backs of his legs. Cohen grabbed him and arrested his fall.

Ammunition was cooking-off inside, every explosion bringing down a lethal shower of broken tiles and flame-blackened glass from the windows.

Their legs wouldn't carry them far, and they gratefully slumped to the ground, as they fought for breath and flapped at the sparks running along the edges of their jackets with bare hands. Behind them the building, flame and black smoke boiling from every door and window, began to fall in on itself, doing so floor by floor like a folding house of cards.

With the settling of the last wall, Revell became aware of something new, alien, and frightening. Silence, almost total silence. It was as if the structure's collapse had marked the battle's crescendo, and signalled its end. There was a horrible sick feeling in the pit of his stomach that had nothing to

175

do with the taste of smoke in his mouth.

"I kinda lost track toward the end." Cohen rung a finger in each ear in turn and flicked the wedges of wax from beneath his short nails. "Those guns have stopped for only one of two reasons. Do we tiptoe away now, or do we go and see who's won?"

When he exerted himself to stand again, Revell was astounded to find that he didn't emit smoke when he exhaled. "On your feet, we're tiptoeing, but toward the main street." The confidence he injected into his words was belied by what he felt inside. Cannon fodder, that was the term that had run through his mind earlier. He was about to find out how near the truth it had been. A call on the radio would have told him at once, but he was in no hurry to find out.

"Better give Casevac the numbers." The major looked at the two groups of wounded sitting, sprawling or lying on the sidewalk in front of the coffee shop. "They'll either have to send a couple of choppers, or work a shuttle service."

The Russians formed the largest group. Under the watchful eyes of Clarence and Andrea they sat still and quiet, those still conscious staring sullenly ahead at nothing, seemingly oblivious to the pain of multiple wounds, including extensive burns and jutting fractures.

"You want me to ask for our chopper now?" Having sent their call sign, Cohen waited for an acknowledgement.

"Not yet. When we've got our casualties away."

176

Revell turned to Libby. "Is this all of ours?"

"Just these six, Major." Taking a safety pin from between his teeth and securing a bandage with it, Libby looked back toward the centre of town. "There may be more, but we can't get to them."

A fierce blaze engulfed several blocks around the scene of the battle. Houses and stores that weren't already alight were steaming in waves of heat. Budingen was being rough dried before being consumed.

"How are they?" Only Kurt's face was recognisable to Revell, the other five were from among Hogg's recruits.

Libby moved out of earshot of the wounded. "It looks to me like three of them aren't going to make it. That includes our Grepo." He wiped blood-smeared hands down the front of his jacket. "There's another, with internal injuries, who'll be touch and go, depends how fast they get him back. The other two will pull through, with luck."

"Right. When you're finished here, you'd better see what you can do for the Ruskies." Revell held up his hand to stifle the expected protest. "I know, that's not your way, but we've been fighting right on the High Command's doorstep. They'll be expecting some live ones, well half-alive. Do your best."

Libby begrudgingly gathered together the various torn strips of tablecloth and the remaining field dressings and went over to the Russians. Andrea stepped forward to stop him as he bent to attend to a senior sergeant who'd lost a hand and a lump of flesh from his side, through which his glistening stomach wall could be seen.

"They will all die soon." She waved her M16 over the Russians. "What can it matter if some die sooner?"

Ignoring her, Libby moved on to his next patient. As he did, the man he'd just attended to tore off the wadding that had been applied to his side, and tried to do the same to the swaddling about the stump of his wrist.

"You see. They want to die, let them."

Another tablecloth fell in strips about his feet as Libby used his teeth to break its hemmed edge. "Why don't you go away and have a bath in blood, or whatever it is you do for enjoyment? Just let me get on with what I've been ordered to do."

Andrea levelled the assault rifle at the Russians, her finger, as always, on the trigger. "We waste time, we should kill them now."

"Not bloody now you don't, not after I've torn up this lot. When I've finished, if the Major says so, you can cut them up with a blunt steak knife, but right now you're guarding them, so just bloody guard."

"What's the body count, Sergeant?" Revell hadn't waited to overhear the outcome of the argument before turning to the NCO.

"Including an estimate of those who never got out of their vehicles, I reckon about sixty, plus of course the Ruskies we've got here; seventy-five in all."

"It looks like a flak-tank and maybe a couple of APCs managed an about turn and are now going hell for leather for the safety of their own lines, but that still leaves a heck of a lot unaccounted for. What would you put it at?"

Hyde had already considered that, and had a guess

ready. "Not too many. These commies are pretty predictable. The majority of those who made it to cover will now be hoofing it as fast as they can for the Soviet side. There can't be above a half dozen still skulking here, and most of those will be the ones too scared even to run."

"Well we'll leave them to others. I expect a few patrols will be along to mop-up any leftovers in the next day or two. If you're right about that armour that got away, I can't see it getting far. They'll either run out of gas, or bump into our forward positions."

"Major," Cohen interrupted, "that Prowler is going home now. He wants to know how we did. You want to speak to him?"

"Yes, give me the set. I've a report to send as well, so I won't be needing you for a while. See if you can give the lieutenant a hand."

Not needing to be told a second time, Cohen wandered off. Keeping at a safe distance so as not to get involved, he watched Hogg supervising the setting out of the landing markers in the middle of the square, for the casualty evacuation helicopters that were due soon.

"I knocked out that one." York indicated a burning T84.

Rocognising it as a tank Hyde had destroyed, Cohen was tempted to say so, but didn't.

"And that one."

York pointed to an APC that Revell had knocked out. The notion that a lesson might be in order, occurred to Cohen. "That's good, very good. But you know you should finish them off a bit neater."

"Neater?"

179

"Didn't you know?" Keeping his own deadpan, Cohen enjoyed the incredulous expression on York's wrinkled face. "When the fires are done the engineers come along and clear the route. Can't leave the place all cluttered up with big black lumps of steel, can we?"

"No?" York wasn't at all sure. "No, I guess we can't. But what's all this about being neater. This some crazy joke?"

"No way. A joke it isn't. Fussy guys these engineers, fussy and tough. If there's one thing they don't like it's having to shift a tank with damaged tracks. Captain I knew did it twice. First time the engineers dumped it in front of his married quarters. He couldn't get his car out for six weeks. The second time it was worse."

"How, how worse?" Incredulity and curiosity mingled in York's face in equal proportion.

"The second time he blew both tracks and half the road wheels off a T84, and made them real mad; so they did it up in brown paper and sent it carriage forward to his home in Burbank. He's still paying, last I heard."

"You're having me on."

"On my life, I'm not." Deciding there was still room to embellish the fabulous tale, Cohen shifted his angle of approach. "Seeing as you're new out here though, maybe I can fix it for you." He gave that a moment to sink in.

"OK, so go on . . ."

It couldn't be that easy. Had he at last found the ultimate sucker in York? Cohen decided to pitch easy this first time, he could try a real wild one later, if this worked. "I've got this brother, he's in the metal recycling business." The continual nodding by York didn't appear to confirm understanding, it was more like confirmation that his basic auditory circuits were still functioning, and he could hear.

"He's got this contract, to clean up the battlefields. At the moment he's in Hamburg, building the biggest mountain of junk you've ever seen, only he can't get any of it out because of the siege."

"So what?" Suspicion was stirring in York's befuddled brain.

"So I'm his agent for the rest of the Zone. For twenty bucks apiece, I can have him tow away your wrecks. Before the engineers arrive."

"You said he was in Hamburg . . ." The suspicion strengthened.

Having stretched York's credulity as far as it was likely to go, Cohen couldn't resist it, he went for bust. "He is, see he's got this big winch, and a special long towing hawser . . ."

"Piss off."

"You blew it money bags." Having sidled closer to listen, Dooley suffered a conflict of emotion as he enjoyed Cohen's failure and simultaneously heard him throw away forty dollars of the inheritance he looked upon as his by right. Well, there was nothing he could do about the money, so he might as well get what satisfaction he could out of the little runt's defeat. "You had him, and you blew it."

Cohen affected indifference. "It's nothing. It was worth it to find out that somewhere in this great big world there is someone even thicker than you."

"You calling me thick?" York bridled.

"Maybe you've got a better word?"

Planting a huge paw in the centre of York's chest, Dooley restrained. "Oh no you don't. You spill a drop of his money and I'll tear your eyes out and use them as suppositories."

"I'm going to twist that lump of shrapnel in Kurt's gut. Anyone going to join me?" Cohen strolled back toward the group of wounded.

"Does he mean it?" Now York was uncertain which of the radio-man's utterances to believe.

"Not in a physical sense." There could be enormous potential for creating aggravation between the little corporal and York, and Dooley's brain was already working overtime, outlining the first few ideas. Given a bit of time, he could arrange it so that York would never believe a word Cohen said. Hell, there was a lot of fun to be had out of this situation.

He was about to put the first into action when Cohen burst into flames. "Where the hell did that come from?" Catching up with the corporal among the wounded, he threw him down and dragged him clear of the phosphorus-spitting grenade.

Another landed among the wounded as York helped scuff the globules of fiercely burning chemical from the deeply burnt flak-jacket.

Clarence and Andrea were both pumping shots at the upper windows of the coffee shop, then they had to jump back as several more of the incendiary bombs landed among the Russians. Others joined in, and, at irregular intervals, still more of the horrific cylinders would tumble out to add their fuel to the smoke-wreathed fires raging among the wounded.

There was no chance of pulling the casualties clear, and those who tried to make it by themselves managed to crawl only a yard or two before the white flames engulfed them. Kurt was briefly visible, sitting up and waving fiery arms, before a long burst from Andrea's M16 pushed him back down.

"Get them, get them." Revell hurdled two charred bodies and plunged into the smoke.

Andrea and Dooley followed, Hyde holding the others back.

"Three's enough. York, Libby, round the back. The rest of you fan out and cover the front. Make sure of positive identification before you fire." Hyde dragged Cohen to his feet, smoke still wreathed from his flak-jacket, his eyelashes and eyebrows gone.

"I'd make a fucking good fireman. Look at the practice I'm getting." Hands shaking, Cohen slowly unfastened the body armour and slipped it off to check none of the pockets had been burnt away. "That's the second time I've been roasted today."

There was a long rattle of automatic fire from the coffee shop and the stabbing flame of a muzzle flash showed in an upstairs room.

CHAPTER THIRTEEN

Through the partially open doorway Revell could see the legs of the Russian infantry officer he'd fired at. The man's calf-length black boots were slashed and punctured by the storm of shot that had torn into him as the 12-gauge assault rifle had blasted him with five fast rounds.

"Keep down." The major had to shove back against Andrea who was standing close behind him. Even here, even now, the close contact with her body felt good. He took a deep breath, another, then jumped to his feet and crashed into the door.

The weight of the body behind it increased its resistance to the charge and Revell felt his shoulder jar at the heavy impact. There was no one else in the room. Two more phosphorus grenades lay on a table, a third near the body, its pin unpulled.

Dooley watched the stairs leading up, while Andrea came in and turned the body onto its back. The powerful cartridges had done immense damage to the Russian's face and torso, and every drop of his blood was draining from the huge rents. "One less."

"Let's check the rest of the building." Stowing the unused bombs in his belt, Revell followed Andrea and Dooley.

Two more rooms on that floor were quickly checked. The method Dooley used was simple, and classic. His hefty boot would batter a door open, and then the blast grenade he'd held with the pin withdrawn for three seconds would be tossed in and the door pulled shut again. Even as the concussion pounded on the wall beside them, he'd leap in and spray sharp bursts into every corner.

Up another flight and three more grenades failed to flush any Russians from hiding.

"This one's mine." Revell stopped beside the strongly locked door that led to an owner's apartment. There were recently made footprints in the dust before it.

"Fire the house." Andrea tapped the head of a grenade protruding from Revell's waistband. "Let them taste the flames."

"You don't give a fuck about revenging Kurt." Dooley fingered the keyhole of the mortice lock. "I suppose you want us to think your bumping him off was done out of mercy, well screw that. You just got mad because you thought someone else had got to him first."

"Stand back." Pushing the others aside with a sweep of his arm, Revell blasted the lock with a single shot.

It swung open, revealing a flight of stairs immediately behind it, with another door at the top.

"You stick your head through that one, Major, and

they'll ventilate it for you. That's just what they're waiting for." Taking out another grenade Dooley tossed it nonchalantly. "How about you blast out the bottom panel and I let them have this, just to even the odds?"

"No . . ." Revell kept looking at the bottom door, the lock had been completely shot away, no wonder it had flown open . . . "No, I've got a better idea. You wait here."

Slowly, ultra-cautiously, the major climbed the stairs one at a time, expecting that at any moment a tread would squeak and the door above would open, to emit a tumbling wood-handled metal cylinder.

He stopped several steps from the top so that his head was level with the bottom of the door, then brought the 12-gauge up to his shoulder.

Suddenly the door smashed open and a hail of fire swept out of the room and over his head. Revell's answering single shot caught a Russian in the act of reloading his AKM and sent him crashing backwards over a low table, dead before he landed.

Worming to the top of the stairs, Revell tentatively opened the door, to reveal a fussily furnished sitting room. There had been two weapons fired at him, of that he was sure, but there was only one body. Where was the other Russian? It could be another trap, an invitation to them all to gather in the room, and present a better target. He signalled the others to wait where they were. Andrea had already mounted a couple of steps, and didn't stop until Dooley caught up with her and held her back.

An inch at a time, Revell eased himself up until he stood on the threshold of the room. Four doors led off, and all were closed. He didn't know what logic or intuition prompted him to first try the door to his immediate left. He crept to it, grasped the satin-finished aluminium handle and barged in, crouching low to present the smallest possible target.

A dozen shots from a 9mm automatic sprayed wildly past him, then the Russian officer threw the pistol itself and bolted for the window. Hurdling the bed he hurled himself at the glass, and it shattered, but that was as close as he came to diving through it and on to the roof of the next building.

Snarled by a net curtain that caught on his every button and buckle the Russian fought to free himself, but it resisted the efforts he made to tear it or pull it down. The harder he tried, the more entangled he became. Though it bowed and the brackets supporting it started their screws from the wall, the curtain rail held.

"You going to finish him, Major, or do you want me to do it?" Standing by the door, Dooley watched the Russian's weakening struggles.

Andrea squeezed past the big man. "I will do it, let me."

"No, cut him down. Our Command are always looking for propaganda, something to counter the lies the commies trot out every day, let's give them a war criminal." Revell stepped aside to let the others reach the trapped man.

A heavy cuff to the side of the Russian's head, delivered by Dooley, put a swift end to his lip-curling invective, and caused him to sag at the knees.

Revell had stooped to retrieve the Stechin pistol when a drawn-out wailing scream flooded the apartment. Dooley and Andrea both stood by the prisoner, both held bayonets. It was the girl's that was smeared with dark blood, stained almost to the hilt.

"What the hell . . . ?"

"She just did it, I couldn't stop her . . ." Only twice before had Dooley seen his officer as furious. "I thought she was just cutting the curtain, like me." The major hadn't blown his top in ages, not since Andrea had joined them, and now the old rage had returned, and it was aimed at her.

"I have no time for trials. This is more sure." She held up the bayonet. "He might have escaped from us, or taken his own life."

"And you thought you'd save him the bother. Listen carefully, when I give an order you follow it." The words were uttered quietly, but carried more menace than if they had been shouted. "If you ever do anything like this again, if I even have reason to suspect that you have, then you go in the cage. When I say I want a Russian kept alive I mean it. There are thousands out there you can butcher, but if I want a prisoner for a special reason, then you leave him alone."

Andrea was considering the threat that had been made. "And how could you have me put in the cage, without making great trouble for yourself?" A small tight smile curled up the corners of her mouth.

He told her, with the same slow deliberation as his earlier warning. "I will tell our Intelligence Service that Kurt told me you were an ex-Grepo, and that you killed him when you found out." He waited for her reaction.

She didn't doubt that he could make the story ring true. He had already woven a tale about her and Kurt to keep them and those same skills could be used to unravel it again. How far could she exploit his feelings for her? Had she already gone too far? Her next words must not be careless, not if she wanted to stay out of the prisoner of war camps . . . the thought of those cages was the only thing that brought her fear.

"I was angry. I saw the look in his face . . . and thought of what he had done, even to his own men . . ." Was it enough? She watched Revell to see if anything had to be added.

God, he wished he could believe her. Anyone else he might have, but not Andrea. Right here and now he had to decide whether or not to keep her. He wanted to; wanted so much more than just keep her near him. And there was the unwelcome complication of Dooley's presence. The big man had faced plenty of charges from him in the past, and received other, more summary, punishments at his hands. If Revell backed down now there was the danger that he'd be seen to be favouring the girl. But damn it he was, always had, though he'd tried not to show it.

"Go and help with the wounded." He made it as sharp as he could, and there was a genuine edge to his words. Damn the girl for putting him on the spot like this. "And I don't want you helping any of them out of their misery."

"Search him for papers." Revell pretended not to see the casual thoroughness with which Andrea wiped the long, thin blade on the dead Russian before going down.

"She's got a nice arse, Major, don't you think?"

"Don't get smart, Dooley. Just give me the papers." He hadn't fooled the big man, but he'd gone through the motions. Maybe now he'd be more trouble to handle away from the Zone. When Dooley wasn't preoccupied with the problems of staying alive on the battlefield, he was every sort of trouble a commander could have. Fights . . . drink . . . women . . . it was as though he was determined to carry as many aspects of the Zone about with him as he could and, by frequently creating mayhem among the military and civilian population, he contrived to do just that. And now for a while he'd be worse, expecting to trade on what he'd just witnessed. Well, perhaps the first couple of times Revell would pedal soft, but after that . . .

"'You want to use those, Major. Be sort of fitting."

Dooley was indicating the incendiary grenades. "Why not? Here, you do it." As Revell left the room, Dooley lobbed a bomb onto the double bed.

The dead body swayed as it hung, moved by the waves of roasting air that surged through the broken window. As the last footsteps the apartment would ever hear echoed back from the stairs, the fine filaments of nylon shrivelled in the heat and finally released the Russian. He fell forward, and one hand flopped out of the window, held there by impaling pinnacles of glass. The fierce gusting draughts from the fire kept it in bobbing motion, and it waved good-bye to the world.

". . . Done to a bloody crisp. Not one of them'll make

191

it to the field hospital, let alone to a burns unit."
Burke watched the pair of scruffy Hueys lifting off,
the late afternoon sun highlighting the faded red
crosses on their cabin doors. "How come you didn't
hitch a lift, you could have played on that?" He
nodded at the wrappings of bandage around Dooley's
leg.

"No way. We're going back bloody heroes. If any
one is chucking forty-eight hour passes about, I want
to be in line to collect my own. I might just get
overlooked if I'm sitting on a bed that stinks of
disinfectant, surrounded by twenty other guys with a
better claim."

"Move it you two." Hyde called from the door of
the Chinook. "We're waiting to lift off."

"On our way, Sarge." There was a loud rush of
wind from Dooley's lower gut. "See, I'm even using
jet propulsion."

The co-pilot greeted them as they boarded.
"Which of you two has pinched a stack of our
decorations?"

The expression on Burke's face was one of genuine
surprise, that on his companion's affected innocence
and ignorance.

"If I had my way I'd leave you here, let you walk it.
Don't take any more or we might put you out yet, at
three thousand feet."

"Touchy ain't he?" Making himself comfortable,
Dooley waited until the co-pilot had returned to his
seat and was busy with the controls before taking out
a wad of crumpled glossy paper from beneath his
jacket. "Hey, look at this one." He held out a full
colour centrefold crotch-shot toward Burke. "She's

192

got a crease right along her crack. Now ain't that something to get your teeth into, or your tongue."

"Wouldn't know, I just fuck them, not eat them."

"Oh boy, are you missing out." Dooley kissed the picture. "A couple of big licks and you can drive them wild, so long as you don't mind getting a few hairs stuck between your teeth. Kinda spoils it if you have to stop to get them out."

"You're warped." The conversation had been overheard by Clarence.

"Yeah, that's possible, but if I am I enjoy it, and it don't do nobody no harm, just the opposite, so what's it matter? Here, you want one . . . oh, sorry, you don't need it, you got the real thing." He made a mock wave to Andrea, and could hardly believe it when she came over to him, and took the page out of his hands.

"You like this?" She took a second illustration, and turned it around several times, uncertain which way up the two girls should be.

"I like the real thing better, but I take what I can get." Continually nudging Burke, Dooley moved over for her to sit down beside him. Her hips needed a surprising amount of space. He tried to imagine her undressed, bent over . . .

"There are things you can show me."

This was getting good, but Dooley wasn't sure how far to go along with it. The sniper was watching and he had a healthy respect for him. He tried to temper the elation he felt, as Clarence turned and went to the back of the compartment.

"So . . . what did you have in mind?" His hand kept hovering over his crotch, wouldn't he have just loved to have shown her, pulled her face down to it. Those bright teeth nibbling at him, yeah, that'd be good.

Sorting through the pilfered pictures, Andrea selected one and showed it to Dooley. "You see this one . . ."

He saw it alright. Dooley could feel sweat pouring off him as he looked at the full frontal black girl, one leg cocked up on a chair, her thighs spread wide.

"How would you do it to her?"

Willing as he was, Dooley could hardly believe what he was hearing. This was too good to be true . . .

"Where would you thrust your bayonet?"

It *was* too good to be true . . .

Revell watched from where he stood beside the radio station. It wasn't possible, she couldn't be switching to that great slob; but there again her first choice of companion had been a crazy one, the loner, Clarence.

"I've got the commander of that blocking force for you, Major." Cohen hesitated before passing over the handset. "You know him."

Revell paid the remark no special attention, until he heard the voice coming over. In fact it wasn't so much that he recognised the voice as the language.

"OK, Colonel . . . Like you say, Colonel, it's a cunt . . ." He jotted down a map reference. "Yes . . . we'll pick you up . . . Glad to hear you got every mother-fucker, Colonel . . . out."

"It was Ol'Foul Mouth then, Major?"

"Colonel Lippincott to you, Corporal. You value your stripes, don't you forget it." But Revell devoutly

194

wished he could. Even talking to the man was an experience, but after the first time the novelty of listening to a tirade of obscenity from a senior officer wore off. Worse, Lippincott expected his subordinates to use "earthy English, something the fucking troops can understand." Revell played safe by throwing his own words back at him. "Here, give this to the pilot, tell him an LZ is already laid. We should see smoke before we get there."

Trust Ol'Foul Mouth to want to get back to his creature comforts as fast as possible. The colonel was always going on about how he longed to get to grips with the "shitty commies," waving the stump of the arm he'd lost in a Russian strafe attack on a forward HQ to emphasise every point. But the immaculate, almost dandified uniforms he sported and the trappings of luxury with which he surrounded himself didn't go well with the blood and guts image he liked to project. It looked as though he'd at last tricked or bullied or blackmailed someone into letting him have a crack. And Revell was forced to admit that if his scratch force had already accounted for the remainder of the column, then he'd done a remarkable job. But there again, it was likely he'd been able to call on more firepower than Revell had . . .

"I've got it in sight now. Looks like someone has been lighting a lot of bonfires."

Revell went forward into the cockpit. About five kilometres ahead, the pale gray band of the autobahn stretched away to the right and left as far as the eye could see. The area surrounding the section they were aiming for was dotted with flickering red flecks.

Thin black fingers rose up into the western sky, brought into sharp relief by their contrast against the reddish dust-filled clouds through which the setting sun was trying to shine.

As they flew closer the fires showed more clearly, revealing themselves to be burning vehicles. Most were on the slip roads feeding a complex intersection with the multilane highway, but there were five actually on it and one or two beyond.

A disc shaped sky-spy sped past the cockpit, provoking a bout of swearing from the flight crew.

"Those fucking things should be made to self-destruct when they've finished a mission, if they can't get them back." The pilot shook his fist after the unconventional miniature craft. "You know, they leave some of them stooging about on auto for an hour or so after they've finished with them, until they drop out of the sky."

The sky-spy executed a precision turn to complete another circuit of the holding pattern it had been locked into. A two-fingered salute from the co-pilot followed the remotely controlled aircraft. "I know of three choppers that have been hit by those flying cow-pats. Nearly brought one of them down, killed a door gunner and started a fire in a cabin."

"We're looking for a service station." Leaning forward, Revell could see the scene of the recent battle through the thin veil of blue smoke hugging the ground.

It looked as if the column had run head-on into a row of hulldown NATO armour, but there had been casualties on both sides. Among the wrecks on the autobahn, he recognised the chunky turret outline of

196

two West German Leopard tanks, as well as three American M60A2 tanks. The engagement must have been a fierce one while it lasted. A line of Chevrolet military ambulances were filling already.

"Hold on, we're going down." As the pilot settled the old Chinook to another fast landing that brought a groan from Cohen, the light began to fade rapidly.

With the whirr of the blades dying to a whisper, there came a violent rapping at the forward door. Libby pulled a fumbling Ripper out of the way and unfastened it.

"Do I have to come looking for you, or are you coming out?"

Revell jumped on to the weed-infested tarmac of a disused service centre. A weighted down white plastic sheet, laid out in the form of a giant "H" crinkled and rucked beneath his boots. The orange smoke candle that supplemented it was hardly needed, with the numerous fires around giving all the information that could be wanted about wind speed and direction.

"They drove straight into our fucking laps. We just sat behind the crash barriers up on the highway there and waited for them." Lippincott was in fine humour, chewing on a fresh pencil. "The last bunch didn't even put up a fight, just popped up and waved their crappy arms. My boys had themselves a turkey shoot. Some of them started pumping out smoke like crazy, but we switched to infra-red and just went on swatting them. We brewed up every last one."

"Looks like you took some casualties yourself, Colonel." The row of flaming armour on the autobahn stretched away like a line of ruddy beacons.

"Shit. Wouldn't have had them if a flight of

commie gunships hadn't pounced just when we were getting down to business and our attention was elsewhere. We got lucky though, the fuckers only made one pass, must have been low on fuel. Had my own command car shot out from under me though. I'll have to find myself a new driver as well, or get the old one fitted with a new leg. Still, there's always a few eggs get broken, it's the price we all have to fucking pay."

Whether he was referring to his driver losing a limb, or himself losing a car, Revell couldn't be sure. Most likely, the loss that concerned Lippincott was that of a driver who'd become used to his peculiar ways.

"Yeah, we did a beautiful job here. Had the shits under sky-spy surveillance from soon after they'd left you, knew exactly where to wait for them." Lippincott spat out slivers of wood and pieces of lead, examined the end of the pencil then went at it again. "I even had a battery of 155mm cannon south of Goldbach assigned to me, to give Blindfire support with rocket-assisted Copperheads, but I didn't use them, didn't need them. Yeah, my tanks did a real neat job, took out all eighteen of those commie wagons in under an hour."

"How many?" It was a superfluous question, Revell knew he'd heard correctly.

"I said eighteen. What's the matter with you, you had your fingers elsewhere when they should have been in your ears?"

"No, my hearing's OK, Colonel, and so is my counting. It was twenty-three tanks that kept going when we hit the rear of the column. If my subtraction

198

is up to scratch as well, that leaves five commie tanks unaccounted for."

"They could still be in there." Lippincott indicated the inky darkness of the Zone, to the east of the autobahn.

"And maybe they're not." Revell was looking westwards, where a broad glowing band across a wide arc of the horizon marked the city of Frankfurt. "And if they're not, then all hell is about to break loose."

CHAPTER FOURTEEN

"They'll do it." Lippincott took off the headphones and handed them to the major. "They don't like it, but they'll do it. As soon as Corps HQ have confirmation the commies are in the city, you'll be given their location and a general nuke alert will be sounded."

"That should keep the civies nicely tucked up underground, out of my way, while I get on with it." And Revell had thought the fighting over! "You're not coming with us, Colonel?"

"You trying to rile me? No I'm not fucking coming. Command want me to take what's left of this rag-bag of armour and do a sweep in the Zone, just in case those commies are still stooging about near here . . . I ain't gonna find the shitty buggers, all I'm gonna do is spend a long uncomfortable night hauling tanks out of ditches and streams and getting bad tempered. One thing's for sure, no crappy arse licker at HQ is going to think to call me off when those wagons do turn up elsewhere."

There was nothing that Revell could say to that. The colonel was most probably right, and agreeing with him wasn't going to help matters. "We'll lift the moment that laser target designator is on board."

"OK, I'll get out of your way." Deliberately not seeing the offer of assistance from Hogg, but looking at him as he turned to use the step, Lippincott paused. "You guys won't have heard. Seems someone stole a general's car today. There's a hell of a witchhunt going on at HQ. Haven't seen a block long, big, black and shiny Caddy have you?"

"Not us, Colonel." Hogg was a shade too fast with the denial.

"Fine, fine. And I know you're telling the truth, Lieutenant, cause you're not smiling anymore." Taking another step down, Lippincott paused one last time. "I've always kinda hankered after a Cadillac. Fact is, I'm so keen to have one, I wouldn't even mind if it'd had a respray."

Hogg and Revell exchanged glances. A voice floated to them from the darkness outside.

"Powder blue would be nice."

"What did happen to it?" Curiosity got the better of Revell, when commonsense told him not to get involved.

It was Burke who'd been listening, and now chipped in. "You want to know about a black staff car."

"I'm not sure . . ." Hogg thought about it. "You know, I can't even remember where I left it . . . Yes, alright, tell me."

"I saw the front end sticking out of an alley in Budingen, after the battle. There wasn't a scratch

202

on it."

"Thank God. For a moment . . ."

". . . but that was all there was, Lieutenant, just the front."

"You know this Colonel Lippincott." Hogg passed his hand over his eyes. "Think he'd like the car by installments? Piece at a time?"

"Don't worry about it. We have other problems at present."

"It's here, Major." Dooley lifted in the laser designator, making light work of the equipment's forty-seven pounds.

"Take us up." Slamming the door and securing it, Revell joined the flight crew.

The pilot's face was just visible, lit by the glow from luminous instruments. "This bus isn't equipped for fancy manoeuvring in the dark. I hope you're not expecting any hot-shot flying."

"No, like before, take it easy. When we find our target you can drop us off ahead of it. From then on we'll find our own transport, and you can go back to hauling freight, if that's what you still want to do."

"You mean I'll be finished? Hey, now that's good news. I've aged ten years today." The pilot touched his face. "Does it show?"

"In this light you look like you died last week."

"Thanks, Major. That was a real tonic."

Above the cockpit the front engine faltered and ran raggedly for a moment. The nose dipped as the co-pilot played with a selection of fuel switches.

"It'll be that pump again." As the engine picked up, the pilot trimmed the Chinook back to an even keel. "Marvellous, isn't it? All day I haul spares for tanks, guns and fixed wing aircraft; best part of a month I've been waiting for this old bus to be fixed."

Cohen squeezed in. "I think this is it, Major." He pointed to a scribbled line of figures on his board. "That's the map reference. There's been no military confirmation, but the civilian switchboards have been jammed for the last five minutes, calls to the army and police."

"Where is this?" Revell took the appropriate map from a rack and checked the references against it. "If it is them, then they're lost, they've screwed up on the last lap."

"What's at this place we're going to; any girls?" The pilot turned the Chinook on to the heading he was given.

"No, it's warehouses, not whorehouses. A nice industrial area, ideal for us. Long straight roads, with plenty of hiding places just off them."

"So long as there's room for me to put down without having my blades play cat's cradles with power lines, I'm happy." As the pilot took the engines up to their maximum revolutions, the whole fuselage vibrated.

Dooley was happy too. Sitting close to Andrea, he could feel the warmth of her body gradually working through the several layers of clothing that separated them. The trembling of the craft made his backside tingle and kept his mind on the lower portion of his anatomy—and hers. He wondered if the sensation did anything for her. It was rather like being inside a giant vibrator . . . now there was a thought. At intervals he would grin and grimace to the others, and nod to the girl as she rested with her head against

204

a stack of empty pallets, mouth slightly open, moist lips framing perfect teeth, her closed eyes showing off the long dark lashes. She was younger than he usually went for, but a couple of quick ones would be so good. He could have murdered Ripper when he disturbed her by sitting down opposite, catching her feet with his.

"Say, that was real clumsy of me. I'm sorry, I truly am."

Andrea's eyes opened and looked at Ripper, and then right through him.

Hell, she was playing hard to get. Still PFC Billy J. Ripper was not about to be put off. Show an interest, that was a ploy that had always worked back home. "You German?" No answer, just the same unwavering gaze from those gold-flecked brown eyes. "You remind me of a girl I used to go with . . ."

"Then you have had one?"

Now why'd she say that, was she getting at him? Heck no. Press on boy, she'll weaken, try the experience trick. "Sure I've had one, had a whole load, why I've . . ."

"Then you had best stay in practice, it would be a shame to see so much talent wasted."

"What are you suggesting then?" He could see the big man glaring at him, as well as that strange limey. What the hell, go for broke, they couldn't do nothing with a couple of officers present.

"I suggest you do what I think you do best, what you have always done, abuse yourself."

"Abuse . . . ? You mean . . . hey, that's dirty." Ripper had never heard a woman talk like that before. Not even Charlene, and she'd been real fond

205

of men, had sampled almost all of them around town, some said even her pa's German shepherd. The big guy was welcome to this one, talking dirty like that. It weren't decent.

Frankfurt was lit up below them. There was no blackout in force, it was only in the Zone that showing a light could bring down death in any of a dozen different forms. Beyond it, the illumination of the towns and cities on either side gave unmistakable warning to any bomber crew that it might have strayed too far from its target, and the gain from a single contrived "accident" could not be worth the dislocation of transport and manufacturing that would come with the inevitable retaliation. But sometimes there were accidents, real ones, and then the hot lines would burn, "arrangements" would be reached, notes exchanged through neutral countries and the incident buried as swiftly as its victims.

The pace was set by the war on the ground, a situation that suited the Russians with the huge reserves of armour and trained manpower they had built up during the sixties and seventies. And it suited the NATO command, all too aware of its relative weakness in strike aircraft after the near destruction of the air-arm at the beginning of the war, when planes and pilots had been thrown away in desperate attempts to stem the communist advance.

There was no traffic on the streets. With the odd exception, every vehicle had been pulled into the side of the road before its driver and passengers had sought the safety of the deep shelters.

The city was like a body that had recently been

taken off a life support machine. All the organs functioned for the time being, but without the brain's direction it would not be long before they faltered and stopped.

"Close as I can figure, we should be about over them now."

"What's our altitude?" Revell leant over the pilot's shoulder to try to read the instrument himself.

"Two thousand. You want me to circle?"

"Yes, and can you take us down further."

Pilot and co-pilot exchanged glances. It was the co-pilot who spoke for them both.

"You know we've got no armour on this tub. All we've got is the flak-jackets we're sitting on, and they're staying there. They can shoot my head off, but I'm keeping my balls."

"Just a couple of passes should do it, then you can drop us and go home."

"OK, a couple, and then off." Pushing the stick forward, the pilot put the Chinook into a steep spiralling dive to twelve hundred feet.

They beat across the industrial estate, over warehouses, light engineering works, a small chemical plant. A man was stationed at every window, every doorway, and still there was no sign of the Russian tanks.

"I know they're down there." Screwing up his eyes, Revell urged himself to greater concentration. "Start the second run."

"Nothing." The pilot took time to look down at the well-lit metalled roads and floodlit storage yards laced with sidings. "Command must have given us the wrong references . . . Shit, no they didn't."

From a service station forecourt gobs of fuzzy bordered luminescence climbed toward them, seeming to travel faster as they approached. A second stream joined the first as it cut the air behind them.

The Chinook's airframe was shaken hard enough to fracture its welds, as the pilots opened the throttles and jinked the chopper away from the chasing tracer.

"The buggers are refuelling." Dooley shouted as he replied to the hostile fire with short bursts from an M60 he held out of the open door. His targets were far beyond the weapon's effective range, and the tracks of the tracer were lost against the service station's floodlit forecourt.

"Put us down as close as you can."

On Revell's instructions, the chopper executed a tight half-turn, came to a dead stop, and went straight down like an express elevator.

First out, Revell supervised the fast disembarkation of the others. Hyde was last, carrying the heavy designator. He waved to the chopper's crew, his words inaudible through the thrashing of the blades above his head, and gave them a thumbs-up.

The pilot didn't have to hear the order, he'd anticipated it as the last of the squad jumped clear. With a rising scream, the high set engines went to full power and lifted the Chinook into the air.

Three hundred feet above the car park in which it had dropped them, the chopper's front engine gave out a series of flame-accompanied bangs from its exhaust stack. Its rate of climb slowed and stopped and it hung there, its underside clearly illuminated by the light from the street lamps.

Tracer flicked past it, one round flashing like a

firework display as it burst against a rotating blade. Another joined it, then a third. Several of the bursts went into the cabin, or bounced from its curved sides, going off at wild angles.

Just when the faulty engine picked up once more, and the helicopter began to lift again, two of the lines of bullets found the front rotor assembly.

Shedding blades and shining lengths of transmission shaft the Chinook staggered, then began to whirl around in a flat spin as it plunged earthwards.

The point of impact was out of their sight, beyond a long low building flanked by rows of hoppers and silos. They heard the crash, and anticipated the bubble of flame that soared and flared briefly in the darkness.

Hyde put his arm out, and held Libby back. "Nothing you can do, not going in from that height."

A shower of fluttering strips of burning paper rained from the sky. Charred pornography, fragments of maps, pages of logbooks made a fiery flurry of litter.

When the last pieces were consumed and their ashes fell and broke on the roads and rooftops, Revell tore his eyes from the scene as the sound of tank engines intruded. "Get on that radio. I want a link with our battery kept open all the time. All of you, stay close, remember our task is to provide covering fire for Sergeant Hyde with the laser, so I don't want anybody starting a shooting war on his own account."

One of the T84s was still at the pumps, its crew working frantically to complete the replenishment and join the other four tanks waiting along the road. The turret-mounted anti-aircraft gun of every one was manned.

While the others fanned out to either side, Hyde and Cohen took up positions among precarious stacks of weathered and much stencilled packing cases in a yard across from the gas station. Checking the laser projector was locked into the correct frequency, Hyde turned on the designator to warm it up.

"I'm ready. One round to start." He settled behind the box and targetted on the T84. This was his own little world, where he could be God. Where he was God, dispensing death with precision. Anything within his field of vision he could destroy. Beside him, Cohen was droning the map reference into the radio; it wouldn't be long now.

Hyde was counting down the seconds. Thirty; the Russian crew had almost finished. One of them threw aside the hose, letting the last gush of fuel spew across the forecourt. Twenty; he'd leave triggering the beam until the last moment. If the T84 had sensors aboard, he'd give its crew no time to act on their warning. Ten seconds; gray smoke spouted from the rear of the vehicle as it began a jerking turn that would take it out on to the road. Switch on . . . now.

High above the city, at the apogee of its soaring, thirty thousand yard trajectory, the rocket-boosted Copperhead artillery shell began its hurtling descent toward its general target area. Its ultra-sensitive seeker instrumentation, activated by the violence of

210

its 7,000g launch, began to search for sources of laser radiation.

Almost immediately, it detected that being bounced from the hull of the accelerating T84. The round checked the frequency code of the emission it was homing on, matched it with its pre-programmed information and deployed its stubby mid-body wings.

Travelling at incredible velocity, the tiny control surfaces only had to move fractionally to carry out the final course corrections and bring it to its target.

The fifty pound high explosive squash-head charge made a direct hit on the turret top beside the gunner's hatch. The metal could offer no meaningful resistance to the forces unleashed against it . . .

As the service station's high set canopy lifted off its girder supports and disintegrated, a roaring fireball engulfed the pumps and seared the front of the workshops behind them. The T84 rolled out of the flames, towing them with it, and minus every external fitting. It struck a row of cars and climbed on to them, bursting out their windshields and crushing their bodywork, before canting over and toppling on to its side.

A river of blazing fuel gushed from its ruptured hull, pouring down drains and into cracked-open inspection covers. Destruction became complete when the first of the underground storage tanks erupted and showered thousands of gallons of fuel across the area.

Tremors shook the ground as petrol ignited in the confines of the drains and sewers. A second storage

211

tank blasted a hole in the forecourt and sent semi-molten brass valves and fittings and jagged lumps of concrete through the walls and roofs of nearby factories.

"They're coming after us." Cohen punched the sergeant's shoulder to get his attention when shouting failed. "Look, they're coming for us."

Closed down, their co-axial machine guns sweeping the frontages to either side, the last four Soviet tanks were bearing down on them. Their leader fired its main cannon, and blasted a SeaLand container truck parked nearby.

"Get me another round." Grabbing the radioman's wrist, Hyde pulled him back down.

Cohen was sending even before the sergeant had finished speaking. ". . . and we need it now, like right now." He sweated as he watched the T84 coming closer and closer. A burst punched through the crates above their heads and his pounding heart recorded every second that passed. Now the lead tank was only a hundred yards away, and he hugged the radio pack to his chest. "Isn't that bloody shell ever coming?"

"Another seven seconds I think," Hyde was perfectly cool, even sparing the time to answer a question to which the radio-man had expected no reply. The hawser-draped hull filled the viewfinder, the tiny green power-pack condition indicator in the bottom left-hand corner of the miniature screen was superimposed on a mud-spattered, crumpled track guard.

The tank burst apart as its own ammunition added its explosive force to the Copperhead's pulverising impact. A blackened torso thudded on to the road, to be crushed by the tracks of the other tanks as they bulldozed past the hulk.

"What are you waiting for? Let's get the hell out of here." Revell grabbed the designator's other handle and, with Cohen following, helped Hyde with it to the wire mesh fence on the far side of the yard.

As they ducked and squeezed through the gap the lieutenant had cut and held open for them, they could hear the packing cases tumbling and splintering before the Russians' unchecked advance.

They were only halfway across the steel stockyard when the leading armour effortlessly flattened the fence. A man shouted and fell as it opened up with its secondary cannon. Hyde caught a glimpse of the machine gun victim's face. It was the Yank with whom he'd shared the boiled sweets.

"Set it up here." Revell darted in behind a huge bright yellow Lancing-Boss forklift, dragging Hyde with him.

"How many rounds?" Kneeling beside them, Cohen was already in contact with the battery.

Hyde stripped the covers from the Hughes equipment. "Four, at twenty second intervals; as soon as they're ready."

The giant sideloader had vast ground clearance, and Hyde took aim from beneath its chassis. Nosing into the yard, the lead tank had slowed to a more cautious pace, but it was still coming on, and now it enjoyed the partial cover of the steel billets and coiled sheet strewn around, as well as the legs of various gantries.

It was the jib of an overhead crane that intercepted the first shot, and as the thunder of its crashing to the ground died away, the second struck a rack of

213

seamless tubing.

A 125mm shell exploded against the far side of the forklift, rocking it on its suspension and punishing the ears of the men in its shelter.

"Bloody hell, they build these things tough." Using his teeth, Burke tied a knot in the improvised bandage he'd wrapped around a gash in his left forearm. "But for Christ's sake clobber that Ruskie next time, Sarge, it might not soak up a second."

Oblivious to everything else, Hyde concentrated on the approaching T84. The tank constantly had to dog-leg to right or left to find a route through the cluttered yard, and each time it did another stack of metal would take it from his sight. It was at such a moment that the third Blindfire round came down, and blasted a tangled pile of scrap.

Revell had already passed the word, and as it emerged unscathed from the smoke the T84 was met by a hail of rifle and machine gun fire and a storm of 40mm grenades. It came on through it all, shrugging aside the puny bullets and suffering no more than loss of paint and damage to some external equipment from the grenades.

All three grenades that Andrea fired struck the vehicle's turret front, and all three exploded harmlessly. She was prevented from firing her last by Dooley.

"Go for the driver's periscope. Blind the fucker."

Taking the advice, and a fraction longer over aiming, she put the next round on to the target, and saw the tank suddenly veer off course and slow.

It was the chance Hyde had been waiting for, and he guided the last of the 155mm shells on to the T84's engine deck. The resulting explosion all but cut the tank in half, and the fire that followed lit the stockyard like day.

Climbing onto the forklift, Revell looked for the last two tanks. Their way blocked by their blazing companion, they had lowered their underbelly blades and were carving a way round it. Slabs and sheets of metal squealed and made masses of sparks as they were rammed and shoved aside. He'd hoped to have bought a longer respite from pursuit, but the Russians weren't letting up pressure for a moment. All day he had been the hunter, now the roles had been reversed, and he didn't like it. Jumping down, he was chased by a long burst of machine gun fire, and as he led his squad at a sprint through the yard the forklift was struck by two shells simultaneously and collapsed onto its nose as one giant wheel was wrenched off, and another flayed and set alight.

Behind them the tank engines boomed louder as they cleared the last obstruction and came on. Ahead of them . . .

"Fucking nothing. It's like the fucking moon."

Dooley's description wasn't far wrong. In front of them stretched a vast tract of reclaimed land, broken only by low hummocks of spoil and a network of deep-gouged tyre tracks. On its far side loomed the towering outline of several cooling towers and the great box-like bulk of a power station. Pylons clustered in front of it, and marched away across the alien landscape.

"Can we make it?"

"We've got to damned well make it. Get rid of anything you don't need." Running across the churned ground was punishing, the ill-spaced ruts left by the contractors' vehicles making it impossible to avoid turning an ankle every dozen steps.

Behind them they left a trail of helmets, flack jackets and binoculars.

"I can hear them." Dooley effortlessly kept pace beside the struggling radio-man. "You sure you don't want to off-load that flak-jacket?"

"Piss off."

"Dooley, carry that radio for him."

"Yes, Major, you bet, Major, right away, Major." Dooley snatched the pack and gloated. "Boy, is this going to cost you. Saving your hide from frizzling back in town, and now portering. Boy, is this going to cost you."

The Russians were playing with them. Clarence didn't look back but he knew that they were. They had the range to shoot them, or the speed to run them down and they were doing neither, just keeping up a couple of hundred yards back. He noticed one of Hogg's men had thrown away his M16. His rifle bumped uncomfortably on his back but he had no intention of parting with it, absolutely none.

Sweat poured into his eyes and Libby could feel every square inch of the lining of his lungs burning, but he wasn't going to drop. Not here, not now. He had to find Helga, had to find Helga ... that thought kept him moving when every fibre of his body screamed at him to stop, give in.

Suddenly, towers of lattice steel were all around them. Transformers stood on thick poles topped by rows of porcelain insulators. They'd been invisible against the black bulk of the power station, still a

216

long way off.

Cables looped overhead, lacing the masses of switch-gear together. There was an unfamiliar smell in the air, and buzzings and hummings and cracklings were all around.

"Keep moving, keep moving." Revell knew the tanks were closing, not willing to carry the game too far in case they lost their prey. "Cohen, call down Blindfire. Everything they've got."

As they emerged from the far side of the complex Cohen tried the set. "It's no good." He swept an arm over the pylons. "I can't get anything near these."

"Then get over there." Indicating a battered car body shell away from the pylons, Revell turned his attention to siting the designator. The only cover for it was a small heap of rubble topped by a sheet of corrugated iron.

The tanks were coming on at top speed now, their tracks sending out twin fans of dirt behind them. They had reached the far side of the power terminal.

"I can't see them." The eye-confusing clutter of the switchgear and pylon legs made it impossible for Hyde to follow the tanks' progress. The first shells were on their way and he couldn't guide them.

"It doesn't matter, just aim in there." The only cover for Revell and the others was the bare ground, and safety depended on how close they could get to it.

The first round hit the top of a pylon, and the flame and roar of its explosion was nothing compared with the terrible chain reaction that started as the severed cables snaked across the bus-bars and switches.

Another round followed, and a transformer burst

217

open, spraying boiling coolant oil over a T84. More shells rained down, dramatically increasing the devastation. Tall pylons twisted and dipped as their legs were cut away, and each one that fell brought down more, the multiple impacts across the terminal producing cascades of sparks that rose like wild fountains.

Air-intake clogged, the saturated T84 stalled. Its driver's hatch opened, then slammed shut as a transformer fell against the hull and flame engulfed the vehicle.

The last tank was still moving, was driving on through the destruction, Copperhead shells blasting the ground about and behind it. As it came out into the open it halted, traversed, and fired its cannon.

Hogg heard the shell pass overhead and explode behind him. A large piece of metal came down amid a shower of soil. He looked up, he knew he hadn't the strength or courage to stand, but he wasn't going to die with his face in the dirt.

High above the T84 a weakened pylon began to buckle, then progressively collapse. It did so with little noise, cork-screwing round as the tension of the cable spans pulled it over. There was a brilliant flash as the high voltage cables fell across the tank, and a halo of blue fire rippled over it.

Slowly, feeling numbed, Revell got to his feet. The ground all around was sprouting other zombie-like figures.

"We made it." Hogg began to laugh. "We made it." The laugher died, but went on inside him, racking his body.

The major felt someone plucking at his sleeve. It

218

was Dooley, tears streaming down his face.

"It's Cohen, he's gone." He fell to his knees and sobbed, holding his face in his hands.

"He's dead?"

"He's gone." Dooley tried to collect himself, wiped his face with his jacket sleeve. "That last shell, there's nothing left of him." He almost broke down again. "All that money, the little shit took it with him."

www.ingramcontent.com/pod-product-compliance
Lightning Source LLC
Chambersburg PA
CBHW031404250626
47155CB00004B/1401